D0438906

FREEDOM'S
PRICE

HIDDEN HISTORIES

FREEDOM'S PRICE

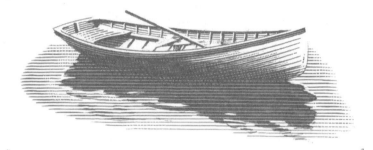

MICHAELA MacCOLL • ROSEMARY NICHOLS

CALKINS CREEK
AN IMPRINT OF HIGHLIGHTS
Honesdale, Pennsylvania

Calkins Creek
An Imprint of Highlights
815 Church Street
Honesdale, Pennsylvania 18431

Printed in the United States of America
ISBN: 978-1-62091-624-7 (print)
ISBN: 978-1-62979-432-7 (e-book)
Library of Congress Control Number: 2015936507

First edition
The text of this book is set in Garamond 3.
Design by Barbara Grzeslo
Production by Sue Cole

10 9 8 7 6 5 4 3 2 1

6056 9588
10/15

For Laney and Jack
—MM

To Harriet and Dred Scott and the many other enslaved parents whose extraordinary efforts protected their children and preserved their families in terrible circumstances
—RN

CHAPTER *One*

Eliza Hates Laundry

WITH A LONG STICK, ELIZA TRACED EACH LETTER CAREFULLY into the muddy bank of the mighty Mississippi River. She darted a glance toward her mother, who was a few feet away stirring river men's filthy shirts in an iron pot bubbling over a wood fire. Ma straightened her back, and Eliza heard her spine crack. It wouldn't do for her to notice Eliza slacking. Or worse, for her to see that Eliza was writing.

Eliza Wants More

"Eliza, what are you doing?" her mother asked. The sharp edge to her voice made Eliza drop her stick and begin to smear the letters back into the mud with her toe. The thick mud stuck to her boot, and she knew she'd never get the smell of decay and dirty water out of them. As fast as she smudged the letters, she wasn't quick enough to evade Ma's sharp eyes.

"Doing lettering out here in the open?" Ma scolded. "What are you thinking? Are you trying to get us in trouble?" Ma wanted Eliza to have an education, but it wasn't safe to let anyone see she knew how to read and write.

Eliza gestured around them. The flat riverbank was deserted. The city of St. Louis and the port lay to the south. North of them was a tangle of shanty houses—but there was no one near enough to see what Eliza was doing. Soon other laundresses would be working nearby at this shallow spot along the river, but for now Ma, Eliza, and little Lizzie were alone. "No one can see, Ma."

"We only have a few weeks before the court decides our case. We can't afford to be careless even for a moment," Ma warned. "Why aren't you fetching more water?"

"I'm waiting for the dirt to settle." Eliza pointed to the barrel that was as high as her waist. It had taken her twenty-three trips with a small bucket to fill the barrel with river water. For a moment, she wondered if Ma hated Mondays as much as she did. Monday through Thursday they did wash at the river for the men who worked on the docks. Friday and Saturday they worked for the Charless family. It was a sorry excuse for a life, doing folks' laundry every day, week in, week out. But Ma never tired of reminding her that they were better off than most colored people in St. Louis. Even if they weren't quite free, they weren't slaves either.

"Let me see." Ma peeked inside Eliza's barrel. She dipped

her hand into the water and lifted it out, letting the water dribble across her palm. Streaks of Mississippi dirt striped across her hand. "It needs at least another hour," she said. "The river is running higher and muddier than usual."

Laundresses in St. Louis didn't have a supply of fresh water for their laundry unless they were part of a proper household with a well. Most used the dirty water from the river or went to Chouteau's Pond where the water was slimy and green. But there was a trick to using the Mississippi River. You had to let the water sit until the dirt sank to the bottom. Then you could pour off the clean water.

Eliza knew a slave named Lucy who had ruined all her mistress's table linens by washing with water straight from the river. She didn't have a mother to teach her how to wash properly. No matter how hard Lucy scrubbed, the linens hadn't come clean. The Mississippi was like that—once it took hold, it never let go. Lucy's mistress had sent her to the auction block the next month, and Eliza had never seen her again. All because Lucy had never learned to let the river dirt settle. Sometimes Eliza thought about Lucy and wondered what had happened to her. The way Ma and Pa talked about the auction block, it was a fate worse than dying.

The Mississippi River held no mysteries for Eliza. She knew all the tricks to doing laundry. But that didn't mean she liked the work. She especially begrudged washing tablecloths from rich white people's dinners. Every gravy stain or smear of meat juice was a promise of a fancy meal that Eliza would never get to eat.

Eliza shifted from one foot to another as she watched Ma consult the never-ending list of chores in her head, considering what Eliza could do with a whole hour. *Please not the men's shirts*, Eliza said under her breath. She hated how the sweat stains had to be scrubbed; the lye in the soap burned her hands and arms. Mondays were bad enough without getting stuck with the worst job.

"I could find some more firewood," she offered.

"We have enough." Ma's tired eyes rested on her daughter, and, to Eliza's surprise, she smiled. Ma's smiles were rare, but they lit up her solemn face and made it beautiful. "I know you don't want to do the scrubbing. I suppose we could make more soap. I don't have much left."

Ma's services were in demand because she was reliable and honest to a fault. But it was her special recipe for soap that let her charge extra. Soap-making was certainly better than pushing fabric against the ridged washboard, which always seemed to scrape Eliza's knuckles.

"I'll do it, Ma," Eliza said eagerly. "Do we got ashes?"

"We *have* ashes," Ma corrected firmly. Ma might not be able to read or write, but she could speak properly. Under her former master, she had served dinner to the most important men in the Wisconsin territory. "But I need some fat. You'll have to go asking."

"I've never gone begging for the fat," Eliza said, her eyes drifting downstream to the deeper water, where the steamboats were moored to the docks. Every boat had a kitchen to provide meals for the crew, passengers, and human cargo. Somehow Ma could always get the cooks to let her have some of the fat drippings.

"Begging, indeed! Mind your tongue, Eliza. They can spare it, and we need it for our business."

Lifting her chin, Eliza retorted, "What business? We work our fingers to the bone, and we don't even get to keep our pay."

"When we win our case, we'll get all the money back. The harder we work, the more we'll deserve our just reward. Don't you forget that." Ma kept her eyes fixed on Eliza until she nodded. "Now, do you want to find some fat or stay here with your little sister and scrub shirts?" Her little sister, Lizzie, was only four, and one of Eliza's duties was keeping her out of the fire and the river.

Lizzie appeared at Eliza's elbow. "Can I go too?" she asked. Over Lizzie's head, Eliza's eyes met Ma's, imploring her to say no. They both knew that Lizzie would follow Eliza anywhere.

"Not now," Ma said firmly. "You have to stay with me."

Lizzie's dark brown eyes, so much like Eliza's own, filled with tears.

"I'll be back soon," Eliza promised, grabbing the pail and hurrying away before Lizzie started to cry.

"Now, mind you're respectful," Ma called after her. "Always ask for the cook. And be careful."

Ma's cautions ringing in her ears, Eliza headed south

along the riverbank to the docks, the pail swinging and knocking against her knees. She intended to enjoy every minute of her freedom; Ma hardly ever let Eliza go out on her own.

Coming from town was a group of colored washerwomen, carrying huge baskets of dirty laundry. They greeted Eliza politely when they passed her on the path. Without even looking behind her, Eliza knew they would say hello to Ma and Lizzie, then walk right by. Ma always worked alone. Ma's skin was as dark as theirs, but these washerwomen were slaves. They were forbidden to associate with the likes of her ma. Harriet Scott was a freedom litigant who had dared to sue her master for her freedom. If the slaves wouldn't talk to Ma, Ma was also cautious about talking to them. Ma never let Eliza forget that the Scotts weren't slaves. It was a shame they couldn't join the others at the riverbank, Eliza thought. It would be easier and much more interesting to do the laundry with a group.

Any day now the court would rule in their favor, and they would no longer be trapped between slavery and freedom. But until then, Ma's rules were Eliza's laws: Don't draw attention to yourself, and stick close to the family. In any case, the court said they couldn't leave St. Louis, so where was there for Eliza to go? Eliza sometimes let herself dream about boarding a steamboat and traveling far away. She wanted to go somewhere she could make a life for herself that didn't involve laundry.

Even with the bucket banging against her knees, Eliza lengthened her stride. The farther she got from Ma and Lizzie, the lighter and more carefree Eliza felt. Ma always hovered, trying to protect her. Eliza was almost twelve and practically free. She strode off down the river's edge, careful not to look too hard for the dangers Ma always warned her about. Eliza Scott could take care of herself.

CHAPTER *Two*

As Eliza drew near the moored boats, the shoreline became busier. The river ran deep here, and the biggest boats could dock close to shore. The wide flat levee between the warehouses and the riverbank looked like a rat's nest of people, animals, and crates. Huge amounts of cargo came in and went out every day in St. Louis. Eliza dodged around porters loading bales of furs and hemp onto steamboats headed north and south on the Mississippi. Other porters were unloading barrels and crates off ships to waiting wagons. The Mississippi River brought shiploads of manufactured goods from the North every day and took back produce and furs from the frontier. Now that gold had been found in California, there were always prospectors heading west. Eliza was glad she didn't see any slaves being loaded onto the boats today. Those slaves would be headed south to hard labor in cotton slave states like Louisiana and Texas.

Today Eliza counted thirty-one boats tied to the docks.

Surely with all these boats, there must be one friendly cook who would take pity on her and give up some drippings.

The first steamboat she tried had a guard who wouldn't even let her up the gangplank. Shrugging, Eliza trudged to the next ship, a bright white vessel with green trim that looked more promising. Best of all, there was no one to stop her from coming aboard. Humming nervously, she headed down the first stairs she could find, knowing that the kitchens were usually in the bottom of the boat.

The luxury in the dining room made her gasp. The tables gleamed like mirrors, and the chairs were cushioned with red velvet. The floor was covered with a thick carpet. She jumped up and down, enjoying the plush feel as she landed. Gingerly making her way across the soft surface, she headed for the swinging door that must lead to the kitchen. She hesitated, took a deep breath, and tapped on the door.

"Yes?" a voice called out.

Pushing the door open, Eliza saw a boy mopping the floor. His dark skin matched her own. He wore an apron streaked with red. Eliza wondered if the stains were meat juice or fruit stains.

"Can I help you, Miss?" he asked. He spoke so softly that Eliza had to strain to hear him. Her nervousness melted away like butter on a summer afternoon. He called her "Miss"! A steamboat like this had lots of paying passengers, and he must have learned long ago to speak politely. Eliza's pa was the same. His respectful manners came in handy at the lawyer's office where he cleaned and ran errands each day.

"I'm looking for the cook," she said.

"He's not here. He went into town for some supplies," the boy answered, leaning on his mop. "Visiting a tavern, more likely!" He winked.

She didn't have much experience talking with boys, but this one seemed to be about her own age and friendly enough. "Can you help me? I need drippings."

"What's a pretty girl like you want with the cook's extra fat?" he asked.

Eliza stared down at the floor. Even though Ma would prefer her to stay a child forever, Eliza knew that young men would start courting her soon. But not yet! "So the cook does have extra fat?" she asked, ignoring the compliment.

"Have you seen him? He's so chubby he can barely fit into this tiny room they call a kitchen."

Eliza couldn't help grinning while she waited patiently for a real answer.

"Yeah, we got plenty of fat," he said. "But only if you tell me what you need it for."

"My ma uses it to make her special soaps," Eliza explained. "We'd be grateful for what you can spare." She held out the empty bucket.

Putting his mop to one side, the young man beckoned her forward. "Come in. What's your name? Mine's Wilson. Wilson Madison." The kitchen was as tiny as he had said. The only fresh air came from a porthole set in the wall above the enormous stove, which took up half the room.

"My name's Eliza," she answered. "Doesn't it get hot in

here?" Her pa always joked that she was more curious than a cat and just as likely to get scalded.

"Hotter than heck," Wilson said, pulling out a huge can full of grease from next to the stove. He poured some into her bucket. "So you're a laundress. Your ma must be a free woman if she's sending you out looking for supplies."

"Not really," Eliza said warily; this was the kind of conversation her mother was always warning her about. She touched the stove gingerly before leaning against it.

"Free or slave—it's one or the other, unless you're running." He lifted his eyebrows, inviting her to explain. "And if you're running, I don't think you'd be making soap."

"My ma and pa lived in a free territory for years, so they're suing their owner for their freedom."

Wilson whistled. "That's brave. Will they win?"

Eliza shrugged. "It's been three years now, and we're still waiting for the courts to decide."

"That must have made your master spitting mad."

"My ma says I don't have a master. I was born on the river."

"A river rat like me!" Wilson wiped stray grease off the side of her bucket with a cloth. "But just because you say you're free, don't mean your master agrees."

"It's the master's widow who claims she owns us. But Mrs. Emerson lives up north in Massachusetts, so we don't ever see her. She hires us out. Ma does laundry, and Pa cleans offices."

"When does your court case get decided?" Wilson asked.

"As soon as the court opens again. Two, maybe three weeks. Then we'll be free." Eliza was surprised at how easily Wilson had gotten her to talk, but she could be just as inquisitive. "What about you?"

"My ma's a free woman in Pennsylvania. She met my pa when he was working on a steamboat. I've been free since the day I was born."

"So you joined a crew too?" Eliza asked.

He nodded. "I love being on the river." He looked out the small porthole. "And I knew what the life was like from my pa."

"I'd love a job like yours where I got to travel all the time," Eliza confided. "The last thing I want to do is what my mother does. Day in, day out, washing other people's underthings is like a millstone wearing me down bit by bit." Her eyes went to the floor as she realized that she'd mentioned underthings.

But Wilson just laughed. "I took this job because the cook promised to teach me everything he knows." Making a show of peering into the dining room to make sure no one was eavesdropping, he added, "If you promise not to laugh, I'll tell you a secret."

Eliza crossed her heart. "I promise."

"I want to be a pastry chef."

"You want to make cakes?"

He nodded. "Cook is teaching me. Meanwhile, I do all the cleaning and dirty work. It's a fair trade for a dream."

He leaned against the worktable in the center of the kitchen. "I've told you my secret—what's yours?"

"What makes you think I have one?"

"Call it a hunch." He grinned widely, inviting her to confide in him.

"I do have a secret wish," Eliza offered. "I've never told anyone."

He spread out his hands.

"Maybe someday I'll tell you," she said with a giggle. "After I know you better."

"Then, I'll have to see you again," Wilson declared.

"On Sundays you can always find my family at the First African Baptist Church on Fourteenth Street and Clark Avenue." She hesitated, then added, "I sing in the choir."

"I'll try to come. Maybe next time I see you, I'll bring you a cake."

"That'd be nice," she said, holding out her hand for her bucket.

"We're sailing north in a few days, but we'll be home soon enough. We have a regular route up the Ohio River to Pittsburgh and back." He put the handle of the bucket in her palm; it was heavy enough to placate Ma when she asked where Eliza had been all this time. "Eliza, it was a real pleasure to meet you."

"Likewise," she murmured. She liked that their eyes were at the same level. Usually she was taller than most boys her age. "Thank you again." Holding up the bucket, she waved.

Eliza was heading back through the dining room when she heard heavy steps coming down the stairs. A man was tripping and swearing as he tried to navigate the narrow stairs. She set the bucket down and ducked behind a velvet chair. Even in the dim light she could see the man was round as a pot of jelly and his face was just as red.

"Who are you?" he demanded loudly, catching sight of her. "What are you doing here?" His voice was slurred, but he was steady enough to grab her. Eliza tried to pull away, but his fingers clamped on to her arm.

"Hey, Cook!" Wilson called from the kitchen. The man turned his head, which gave Eliza the opportunity to twist out of his grip. She grabbed the bucket, ignoring the sloshing and spilling of the grease, and ran up the stairs as fast as she could. She flung herself headlong down the gangplank, letting the heavy bucket help pull her to the shore. Gasping for air, she glanced back at the ship. All was quiet. Maybe Wilson hadn't gotten into trouble for her sake.

Instead of heading back to Ma, Eliza took a dozen steps in the opposite direction so she could see the name of Wilson's ship. It was the *Edward Bates*. Eliza would keep an eye out for the *Edward Bates*—she wouldn't mind meeting Wilson again.

CHAPTER *Three*

No NEED TO HURRY, SINCE THE ONLY THING WAITING FOR ELIZA was a mountain of dirty clothes. She walked slowly down the shore, lost in a pleasant daydream of Wilson coming to church with a cake. Ma would be suspicious; she didn't trust any boys. But she'd be won over by his good manners. Lizzie would love him because he'd brought a treat. And Pa would like anyone who made Lizzie smile.

A toot from a passing steamboat brought her back to herself. With her free hand, she waved as the boat moved majestically down the river. It was coming from the North: Where had it been? What kind of people was it carrying? What was its cargo? Eliza never tired of watching the massive paddle wheels go round and round, dripping water in the ship's wake.

The spring air lost its chill as the sun climbed in the sky. The bucket dragged in the dirt; drippings were heavier than they looked. But Eliza paid no attention. Instead she practiced a hymn she had learned at church. Happy or scared, Eliza loved to sing. She cast her voice out toward the center of the river and then let it drift back like a fishing line.

I've got peace like a river in my soul,
I've got a river in my soul,
I've got joy like a fountain in my soul,
I've got a fountain in my soul.

In the distance she saw the steam rising off Ma's laundry kettle, taking a fantastic shape for an instant, then disappearing in the breeze. Bustling about the fire, Ma was easy to make out in her bright green cotton dress with a white apron. The same colors, Eliza thought, as the *Edward Bates.* Slaves usually wore a dull, faded blue, and no doubt Ma's mistress, Mrs. Emerson, would take issue with Ma's choice of color. However, since Mrs. Emerson was far away in Massachusetts, Ma could do as she liked. But her dress was still made out of cloth that marked Ma as a slave. If only the court would hurry and make up its mind—then Ma would be free to wear any color, any cloth, she pleased.

In the distance, Eliza could see the other laundresses chatting and working together. The only person who seemed out of place was a colored boy hanging about the riverbank between Ma and the others. Not many boys helped with laundry. His short trousers and too-big linen shirt made it hard to gauge his height. She wondered who he was. If he was a slave, his master was too miserly to buy him boots. As he roamed along the bank, eyes fixed on the ground, Eliza decided he must be from the shantytown. The people who lived there were always scavenging for anything they might find along the riverbank.

Eliza watched Ma lift the laundry with her long paddle, then push it back into the boiling water. She knew how heavy the wet clothes were, and she winced to see how Ma braced the small of her back with one hand as she stirred. It was odd that she hadn't noticed before that Ma's back hurt her. Maybe Ma just never let her go far enough away to see things in a new light.

Lizzie was throwing a small wooden ball into the air and laughing out loud. Her little sister was so easy to please. The whole family loved to make her happy. Ma would scold and say they were spoiling her—but as soon as Ma heard Lizzie's gurgling laugh, she would smile too. Take that ball, for instance. The delight on Lizzie's face when Pa gave it to her had cheered everyone for days. Eliza smiled as Lizzie caught the ball once, twice . . . on the third throw, Lizzie missed. Faster than Eliza thought possible with her short legs, Lizzie ran after the ball, much too close to the river's edge.

The river looked like it ran slow, but its current was swift and hidden. Eliza's eyes darted toward Ma, but she was too intent on the laundry to notice that Lizzie was in danger. In a split second, Eliza dropped the bucket and ran for Lizzie, shouting her name. Ma heard and whirled around, eyes searching for her little girl. Eliza was closer, and she scooped up her baby sister in her arms and started back toward Ma.

"You scared me half to death," Eliza said sternly. "You can't swim yet, and the river could take you away so fast that I wouldn't reach you in time."

"But I didn't fall in," Lizzie protested.

"That won't matter to Ma." Out of the corner of her eye, Eliza noticed the boy with short pants had started toward them, then stopped short. Perhaps he had wanted to help.

As Eliza had predicted, Ma had some sharp words for Lizzie. "I should tie a rope around your waist and tie the other end to my ankle," Ma threatened.

Lizzie cowered away from Ma, clinging to Eliza's leg.

"You wouldn't really do that, would you, Ma?" Eliza asked.

"If Lizzie can't stay away from the river, I'll have to."

Lizzie began to cry, big fat tears rolling down her cheeks. Ma and Eliza exchanged frustrated looks—neither of them could resist Lizzie when she cried.

Ma knelt down and gave Lizzie a quick hug. "Stop crying and help your sister with that heavy bucket."

Eliza's head snapped toward the abandoned bucket. "C'mon, Lizzie." Eliza let Lizzie tug on one side of the bucket while Eliza did the heavy lifting. As they made their way back from the river's edge to Ma's fire, Eliza slowed down her long stride to match Lizzie's tiny steps.

When Ma turned away from the fire to fetch more wood, a rapid movement caught Eliza's attention. The boy had darted toward Ma's pot, as though he had been waiting for the chance. He grabbed one of the shirts straight from the boiling water, even though it must have scalded his hands. Before Ma even knew what had happened, the boy was running away, toward Eliza and Lizzie.

"Stop, thief!" Eliza screamed, moving to block his way. "Give that back!"

Ma spun around.

The boy hesitated only a scant second, trapped between Eliza and her ma. Then he took off inland toward the maze of ramshackle huts of the shantytown. Eliza dropped her bucket, ignoring the fat sloshing over the rim, and raced after him.

"Ma, get Lizzie!" she called.

"Eliza, come back. Come back right now!" Ma shouted.

She ignored her mother's calls and chased the boy even faster. Ma couldn't afford to replace that shirt. And if they lost their customers, how would the family survive? The thief wasn't burdened with heavy boots, and his trousers didn't catch on the brush like her dress did. The big shirt spread out behind him like a kite catching the wind; Eliza hoped it would slow him down.

They were deep in the shantytown. Eliza wasn't allowed to come here, but she knew what it was. The houses were flimsy, made of materials washed up by the river. But what the river gave, it also took away. These settlements flooded all the time, and the poor people who tried to live here lost everything over and over again. Ma called the shanties dens for thieves. But Eliza had seen her share of criminals, and she wasn't afraid. Not too afraid.

Her legs were longer than the boy's, and she was gaining

on him. But she was running out of time and distance; he knew the area and she didn't. She'd lose him for sure if she didn't act fast. Her breath rasping, heart pounding, she forced her feet to move just that much quicker. In a final burst of speed, she extended her arm and grabbed the back of the boy's shirt. With the strength she had earned by hauling laundry day in and day out, Eliza pulled him so hard he fell. The shirt flopped to the ground.

"Gotcha!" In an instant, Eliza straddled him, her palm flat on his chest to keep him down.

"Oh!" She pulled her hand away from his shirt as though it were scalding hot. "You're no boy!" Besides the beginnings of breasts under the thief's shirt, Eliza now saw that her features were softer and rounder than most boys'.

"So?" the girl snarled.

"You're right," Eliza agreed. "Boy or girl, how dare you steal from my ma!"

Eliza's hand was still raised, and the thief's eyes were fixed on it, her body stiff as though braced for a blow. The girl's ebony skin was marked with pox scars, and her lip showed a recent bruise. Slowly, Eliza lowered her hand.

"I won't hurt you," Eliza assured her. She grabbed the wet shirt, no longer steaming hot, and climbed to her feet. "But this belongs to us."

The girl's eyes widened. "Ain't you gonna turn me in to the police?"

"Not if you never come round my ma's laundry again," Eliza growled. "Why'd you steal it anyway? This wouldn't fit you in a hundred years!" She struggled to fold the shirt over her arm, but it was heavy with water and hard to handle.

"I was going to sell it," the girl replied. "And get some food for me and my ma."

Eliza's stomach let out a hungry growl. Her eyes met the girl's, and they both smiled a little. The shared glance was just enough to bridge the gap between them. "I know what it's like to be hungry too," Eliza admitted. "What's your name?"

"Celia."

"I'm Eliza. Are you free folk?"

"For all the good it's done us." Celia spat out the words. "We're worse off than we was before. Ma's master freed all his slaves in his will. But now we don't got a home or anyone to make sure the catchers don't take us." She looked curiously at Eliza. "What about you?"

"My ma was born a slave, but she's gone to the law to get free. In the meantime, she does laundry." Eliza lost her grip on the heavy shirt, and the girl caught it before it fell to the ground again. Without thinking, Eliza snatched it back.

"I wouldn't steal from you again," Celia insisted with an injured look.

"Come back with me and apologize to my ma. Ask her for help. We don't have much, but we can probably find you a dress and shoes to wear." She glanced down at Celia's ragged pants and dirty bare feet.

"We don't need your charity," the girl muttered.

"You'd rather steal?" Eliza asked, raising her eyebrows

like Ma did when she didn't believe Eliza. "I have another idea. Come to Reverend Meachum's church on Fourteenth Street. He'll help."

Celia stared for a moment, twisting her hands together. Eliza saw that they were covered with insect bites and infected cuts. "I can't."

"Why not? What harm could it do?" Eliza tried reasoning with her.

"I've got to go," Celia blurted. Without looking back, she ran into the tangle of huts and disappeared. Eliza decided she had best head right back to the river before Ma had a fit.

Retracing her steps, Eliza was surprised to see how far she'd run. She couldn't wait to see Ma's face when she returned triumphantly with the shirt, even if it was covered with dirt.

Ma, face stern and arms crossed, was waiting at the river's edge. Lizzie sat on a rock, Ma's usual punishment whenever she got into trouble. Lizzie's mouth fell open as soon as she saw what Eliza was holding.

"Ma, look! I got it," Eliza crowed.

"You disobeyed me. I told you to come back, but you kept on running." Ma's voice was filled with anger. But Eliza could hear the fear too. Her triumph faded, replaced by guilt.

"You're a young colored girl with no one to protect you!" Ma went on. "A slave catcher could have swooped you up, sold you downriver, and we'd never hear from you again. I didn't raise my daughter to be a fool."

Tears springing to her eyes, Eliza held out the shirt. "But I got it back, Ma!"

Without softening one bit, Ma pointed at Eliza, then the shirt. "To us you are worth more than one hundred times that shirt! Don't ever do anything like that again."

Eliza swallowed big gulps of air, trying to keep from sobbing. "I won't, Ma."

Ma glared at Eliza for a long moment.

"I really am sorry," Eliza said.

Ma lay the back of her hand against Eliza's cheek. "You're safe only when you're with us."

Ma's hand was rough from too much lye, but Eliza leaned in to take comfort from it. The memory of Celia, flinching when Eliza held up her hand, flitted into her brain. Neither Ma nor Pa had ever struck her, and Eliza knew they would die to protect her. "I promise to be more careful, Ma," she vowed.

Sniffing hard to keep her nose from running, Eliza shoved the shirt back into the steaming pot of water. With Ma's long paddle, she poked the shirt until every bit of cloth had disappeared under the roiling bubbles.

CHAPTER *Four*

On Saturday Eliza helped her mother at the Charless family's place, a fancy house in the center of town. The Charlesses had at least a dozen rooms to live in and a large garden in back. The house had its own well, so getting clean water was easy. Ma had set up her pails in the basement with doors open to the back garden. The basement smelled of damp and starch, but the garden was fragrant with beds of herbs and early vegetables. Naturally, Eliza preferred to be outside.

"Take those dresses . . . ," Ma instructed. Her voice was muffled because she was bent over a washboard, pushing the heavy cloth across the board. As she pulled the laundry back, she found breath enough to finish her sentence. "And hang them up outside."

Eliza gathered the slaves' wet dresses in a basket and heaved the basket onto her hip. Someday she'd like to use the scales outside one of the big stores and see the difference in weight between a wet dress and a dry one. At least here at Miss Charlotte's house, she only had to haul them twenty feet or so between the basement and the garden. But Eliza missed the breeze from the river and the never-ending parade of steamboats to entertain her as she worked. An enclosed garden meant that the garments could be safely hung to dry without fear of thieves. Eliza was reminded of Celia; she wondered if the girl would come to church the next day. Eliza lifted one dress and draped it over a lilac bush. Her back to the garden gate, she carefully arranged the skirt to lie as flat as it could. The more attention she paid to the drying, the less ironing she would have to do later.

Eliza had just registered the sound of footsteps in the alley beyond the garden when the gate behind her was shoved open without any warning. Eliza tottered, then lost her balance. With a thud, she landed in the dirt.

"You're blocking the gate!" a sharp voice shouted down at her. A pair of high-heeled boots was planted in front of her face. She looked up to see Miss Charlotte's son, Mark, towering over her. She'd seen him once or twice before, but he had never bothered to notice her. She scrambled to her feet and saw that her eyes were level with his. Maybe he wore those boots to make up for not being very tall. He was not yet twenty, but he had the bad manners of someone who had been practicing a lot longer.

"Sorry, I was doing the laundry," Eliza muttered, her face hot. He was the one who had knocked her down, and yet she was apologizing.

"My mother's slaves are as clumsy as they are slow," he barked. Pushing her aside, he slammed the gate and headed to the kitchen door. His mincing walk made him look as though he were skipping on hot coals.

Eliza glared at his back and clapped her hand over her mouth. Ma had told her again and again to hold her tongue. She glanced at the basement door, wide open to let in light and air, hoping her mother had heard how well-behaved Eliza had been. But Ma was still scrubbing in the basement. Eliza's only witness was Lizzie, sitting in the grass trying to coax the house cat to play. Lizzie frowned and said, "That man is mean."

"Hush, Lizzie." Eliza put her finger to her lips. "We can't say so. Even if it's true."

Her fall had torn the sleeve of her dress from the bodice. This dress had already been mended too many times. Even Ma's clever sewing couldn't repair it again. She wished now she'd spoken her mind to Mark Charless.

With a sigh, she returned to the laundry. Once the lilac and forsythia bushes were covered with skirts, Eliza had to make use of the wires strung between two poles. The clothesline was always her last choice because the wire was sharp and hurt her hands. She reached up to pin a dress to the clothesline and smiled. A few months ago, she had needed a stool to reach it. Eliza had no head for heights, even ones that weren't very high. Then she thought of Ma, and her smile disappeared. The taller Eliza got, the more Ma worried about slave catchers. Ma said they looked for girls Eliza's age because they fetched such a good price. As if Eliza would ever let herself get taken by the likes of a slave catcher.

To take her mind off such an unlikely possibility, she began to sing one of the new songs she had heard on the street. She liked it because the words were so funny.

> *I come from Alabama,*
> *With a banjo on my knee.*
> *I'm going to Louisiana,*
> *My true love for to see.*

> *It rained all night the day I left,*
> *The weather it was dry.*
> *The sun so hot, I froze to death,*
> *Susannah, don't you cry.*

Within a few minutes, she had fallen into a working rhythm and almost all the laundry had been hung.

"Hi, Eliza." A soft voice came from the parlor's wide window, opened fully to let in the air on this breezy day. It was Sadie, the cook's daughter. She wore a crisp white apron over her neat blue dress made of shirting, the same kind of dress that Eliza was hanging to dry. It might be a slave's dress, but it fit Sadie well. Eliza couldn't help wishing for a dress that gave her room to breathe. Her own dresses stretched too tight across Eliza's shoulders. She couldn't swing her arms wide, much less run freely.

"Hi, Sadie," Eliza called back.

"You've got the prettiest voice," Sadie said. "The old lady was all crotchety until she heard you singing—then she settled right down."

"What old lady?" Eliza asked.

"Miss Sofia, the master's aunt, just came to live with us. She's a little . . ." Sadie tapped her head. "Your singing kept her still while I brushed her hair."

Eliza ducked her head. She loved to sing, but she wasn't sure it was right to be proud of something the Lord had given her.

"Come round to the kitchen after. My mama's made shortbread."

"I will," Eliza beamed. Working for Miss Charlotte meant treats from the kitchen. Sadie's mother was one of the finest bakers in town.

Eliza's work let her see through the wide window into the grand house. She watched Sadie and the other house slaves polishing Miss Charlotte's prized wood furniture and sweeping the floors. They were chatting and laughing. Their work looked easy. Eliza glanced down at her hands, raw and chapped from the wet laundry. Ma always talked about being free like it would solve all the family's problems, but so far as Eliza could tell, freedom meant more work and less food. *Look at Celia*, she thought. Freedom hadn't helped her at all—she had to steal to eat. But Sadie, a slave, was plump and had a soft life. Sadie didn't have to worry about slave catchers kidnapping her off the street. If you were properly owned, you were protected.

Eliza gave herself a sharp shake; Ma would be furious

if she ever heard her say such things.

Her mind on other matters, she didn't notice when her hand slid along the sharp wire. A thin red line appeared. She stared at her palm, wondering why it didn't hurt. Then the pain arrived. "Ow!" she cried.

Ma was out of the basement like a shot.

"What happened, Eliza?" she asked, breathless.

"It's nothing, Ma." The blood seeped through the cut, like a pool of water oozing up through the mud on the riverbank.

Ma clamped Eliza's other hand over the cut. "Never mind, I know what happened. You were daydreaming or singing instead of paying attention to your work. Go inside and wash your hand at the kitchen pump," she ordered.

"But I'm almost finished," Eliza protested.

"Miss Charlotte's the kindest woman in St. Louis, but if you bleed on her laundry and we have to do it again, she won't pay us twice." She gave Eliza a gentle push. "Now go. I'll finish up."

Eliza made her way into the kitchen by the side door. The smell of bread dough, yeasty and full of promise, filled her nose. Eliza loved the whitewashed walls and the wide, perfectly clean tiles on the floor. Everything was square—the stove, the table, the cupboards—all except Cook, who was round as one of her famous rolls. Her forehead beaded with sweat under her kerchief, Cook was pummeling the bread dough with her fists. Cook looked up. "What is it, Eliza?"

Wordlessly, Eliza held out her hand, palm up.

"Child, let's wash that." Cook ushered Eliza to the sink

and began to pump water over the deep cut. "How did it happen?"

"I sliced it on the clothesline."

Cook shook her head. "You're not the first to cut yourself on that wire."

Eliza jumped as the cold water flooded the cut. To take her mind off the sting of the water as it hit the wound, Eliza asked, "Who did the laundry before us?"

"The house did its own laundry. But one day Miss Charlotte said it was your ma's job."

"Weren't there enough people to do the work?"

"More than enough." Cook shrugged. "But we do what Miss Charlotte says. Besides, ain't nobody gonna complain about doin' less work." She found a clean rag in her pantry and wrapped it tight around Eliza's hand. "Now, sit and hold your hand above your heart. That will slow the bleedin'."

Obediently Eliza lowered herself onto the stool and propped her arm up high on a shelf. It was a relief to be off her sore feet. She wished Ma could rest too, but Ma refused to take a break during the workday. "You get nothing in this world by coddling yourself," she was fond of telling Eliza. Touching the bandage gingerly, Eliza thought a little coddling wouldn't do her any harm.

The kitchen shared the wall with the parlor, and she heard a murmur of voices. The servants who had been cleaning the room scurried into the kitchen like mice fleeing a cat. For the brief moment the door was open, Eliza heard Miss Charlotte saying, "I've made my decision. The answer is no." Her voice was in that spot between impatient and angry.

Sadie spied Eliza and came over. "It's Mr. Mark," she whispered. "He's asking for money again."

Eliza made a face at the mention of Mr. Mark. She wouldn't soon forget how he'd knocked her down and treated her like the dirt under his high-heeled boots.

Cook, who was as curious as she was round, casually went to the door and nudged it open an inch so they could hear.

Mark sounded like a whining child wheedling for a treat. "Ma, I can't go unless you help me."

"Then you shouldn't go, Mark," Miss Charlotte said patiently. "There is plenty for you to do on the farm. It wouldn't hurt you to spend some time out of the city doing some real work for a change."

"I don't want to work on the farm! I want to go west with Frank Sanford. The farm will never make me rich—but in California there's gold lying about in streams for the taking."

California! Eliza had been hearing about life on the frontier her whole life. Ma and Pa had met when their owners were stationed at a fort in the Wisconsin territory. Their stories of those times were mostly sad ones of hunger, cold, and crushed hopes. The only folks who had fared worse than the settlers had been the Indians. And the tales from far-off California were just as tragic.

"If something sounds too good to be true, it usually is," Miss Charlotte replied sagely.

Eliza almost nodded in agreement; Ma liked to say that too.

"I've talked to men who've seen the gold. And touched it," Mark insisted.

"And does it just leap from the river into your hands?" Miss Charlotte asked. "It's backbreaking labor to mine gold, and you've never done a hard day's work in your life."

"I'll show you I can do it," he persisted. "Just give me five hundred dollars, and I'll repay you tenfold when I strike it rich!"

"You're a foolish boy," Miss Charlotte said dismissively. "Besides, I don't have that kind of cash lying about to just hand out for the asking. Now let me be while I talk to Cook about dinner." Sadie hurried out of the kitchen through the other door before Miss Charlotte appeared.

Miss Charlotte was a handsome woman even though she was almost forty. Her spine was so straight, Eliza wondered if she had a steel rod in the back of her dress. She wore her thick dark hair, only slightly streaked with gray, gathered in a bun at the back of her head. Her husband traveled all the time so she was in charge of everything. Her slaves liked her, though she was strict. No one ever crossed Miss Charlotte. Except her son.

But Mark wouldn't give up so easily. He followed his mother into the kitchen. Eliza pressed herself into the corner, wishing she were shorter and less noticeable.

"Maybe you don't have money," Mark went on, relentless. "But you have far more slaves than you need. Just give me one of the breeding females to sell. You won't have to do a thing."

Eliza glared. Mark looked like a gentleman with his dark tailored suit and his black hair carefully arranged across his brow, but he talked about slaves as if they were animals.

"Absolutely not," Miss Charlotte cried, her face flushed. "Our slaves depend on us to take care of them. That's how my father raised us."

"That was thirty years ago on a plantation in Virginia," Mark countered, rejecting the past with a wave of his hand. "It's not the same here."

Eliza cocked her head. She'd never heard that Miss Charlotte's family came from Virginia. Pa was from Virginia too, long ago.

"Our values don't change because we move," Miss Charlotte said.

"The family was quick enough to sell slaves when we needed money."

"But I don't need the money," Miss Charlotte reminded him. "You do."

"But, Mama—this means everything to me! Just give me one." He pointed at Eliza. "That one would do. She's old enough to fetch a good price."

Before she could stop herself, Eliza stood up and spoke for herself. "Miss Charlotte doesn't own me. No one owns me!"

Cook gasped. Despite Miss Charlotte's frown, Eliza repeated loud and proud, "No one owns me."

CHAPTER *Five*

"Eliza, be quiet," Miss Charlotte said. Turning to her son, she said in a casual voice, "She isn't one of my slaves."

Mark raised his eyebrows. "Who is she, then?"

"That's none of your business," his mother snapped.

Mark's eyes darted between his mother and Eliza. "Mama, what are you hiding?"

"All that matters is that Eliza is not mine to sell." Eliza was glad to hear the steel in Miss Charlotte's voice. "In any case, my slaves aren't livestock to be sold on the block. Sometimes we've had to sell some of our slaves, but we always found good homes for them."

They aren't extra kittens from a litter, Eliza thought. *They're people!*

Mark made an exasperated noise. "Like Dr. Emerson?"

"What are you talking about?" Miss Charlotte asked cautiously.

"We sold a slave to Dr. Emerson, didn't we?"

Eliza stepped backwards, speechless. Her father had been sold to Dr. Emerson.

"So?" Miss Charlotte's hand went to the limp lace at her throat, and she darted a glance at Eliza.

"That slave is suing Emerson's widow for his whole family's freedom," Mark said.

With a slight shake of her head, Miss Charlotte said, "My father sold Dred Scott years ago. This doesn't concern you."

"That's where you're wrong, Mama!" Mark said. "My friend Frank Sanford is the one I want to go to California with. He's Mrs. Emerson's favorite nephew. She told him that if she could sell her slaves, she'd stake him for our trip to California. But she can't sell or profit by them while she waits for the court to decide. So she isn't able to give Frank the money. It's not fair." Mark paced back and forth in the kitchen at an angle, making the square room seem half the size. Eliza pressed herself into the corner, but she made sure not to miss a word.

Miss Charlotte started to answer him, but she was interrupted by a knocking at the front door. A moment later Sadie appeared and said, "Miss Charlotte, it's Miss Robinton. I showed her into the parlor."

"I'll be right there," Miss Charlotte said. Turning back to Mark, she said, "You'll have to find the money somewhere else." She swept out of the room, her long skirt swishing along the wooden floor. To Eliza's dismay, Mark stayed behind.

He looked at Eliza like a good housekeeper examines a joint of beef at the market. "Why is my mother protecting you?" he asked, moving toward her.

Crossing her arms across her chest, Eliza didn't say a word.

"What's your name?" He shoved her into the wall.

"Tell him, Eliza," Cook said.

"I'm Eliza Scott," she mumbled.

He took a step back in surprise. "Dred Scott's daughter?" He rubbed his chin. "You're one of the Emersons' slaves."

"I'm not a slave," Eliza retorted.

"You are as soon as the judge throws your case out of court," Mark fired back. "Then Mrs. Emerson can sell you and give the money to Frank. And I'll be able to go to California." He rubbed his hands together.

Despite the heat of the oven, Eliza's skin prickled with goose pimples. A few minutes ago, the cut on Eliza's hand was the worst problem she had—how had danger come so quickly?

Sounding braver than she felt, Eliza replied, "But until the court decides, no one can touch us!"

Mark's weak mouth twisted into a sneer. "We'll see about that," he threatened.

Eliza clenched her jaw to keep her chin from trembling. Mark Charless didn't really have any power over her—no matter what he said. She managed to meet his eyes squarely and not blink. Finally, with a grunt, he turned on his heel and stomped out of the room.

Sadie emerged from the shadows behind the swinging door. "Eliza, you're in trouble now! Mr. Mark is as mean as a rabid dog," she said.

Eliza sank back down on the stool and tried to catch her breath.

Cook's face was grim. "Sadie, be respectful. Mr. Mark would send you to the block as soon as look at you." She turned to Eliza and shook a floury finger at her. "And you, Eliza. Your ma taught you better than to talk back to the likes of him."

"I only answered his questions," Eliza protested, rubbing her breastbone where Mark had pushed her. "You won't tell Ma, will you?"

"Just stay out of his way until he goes to Californy." Cook lifted her dough in both hands and slammed it against the table. "Your ma's heart'd break if anythin' happened to you."

Eliza nodded. She promised herself that in the future she'd keep her head down and her mouth shut. She slipped out of the kitchen and joined Ma and Lizzie in the basement. When she was with them, she could forget about Mark Charless.

Ma didn't seem to notice anything was wrong. She set Eliza to stirring the latest batch of soap even though Eliza only had the use of her right hand. She kept her bandaged arm pulled up on her chest, but it still ached. The heat rising from the fire Ma had built just outside the basement door made the sweat run down her face and into her eyes. But Eliza didn't complain. She deserved to suffer. How often had Ma warned her about drawing attention to herself?

Ma added handfuls of dried lavender from the garden to the soap.

"That smells nice," Eliza said.

"Miss Charlotte likes her laundry scented," Ma answered.

"Even the servants' clothes?"

"For that soap, we'll add lemon balm. There's plenty of that in the garden."

Eliza knew the servants' soap would still smell better than the soap Ma made from fat drippings. *When we win our lawsuit, what will our clothes smell like?* Eliza wondered.

Before Ma could disappear back into the cellar, Eliza seized the opportunity to ask, "Ma, why didn't you tell me that Miss Charlotte's family owned Pa once upon a time?"

"Who told you that?" Ma asked.

"I heard it in the kitchen," Eliza answered with a half-truth. "Why didn't you ever tell me?"

"You didn't need to know," Ma replied, her voice tinged with warning. "It was long ago, and it doesn't matter now."

"But it does matter." Eliza's curiosity was stronger than her sense of caution. "Miss Charlotte gives us this work because she knows Pa, right? Cook told me that the house servants used to do the laundry. Why hire us when she has plenty of people to do it for her?"

"Because I'm one of the best laundresses in the city. That

soap you're making is my own special recipe—no one else has it."

"But . . ."

"Hush, Eliza. Miss Charlotte's business is her own." Ma turned her back on Eliza.

Eliza wiped the sweat from her forehead and sighed. If Ma didn't want to answer questions, she wouldn't. Luckily Eliza could ask Pa later.

Finally Ma agreed that the soap was done to her satisfaction. Eliza carefully packed it into three brown clay jugs and placed the jugs on a shelf in the basement. Eliza's last task was to empty out her washing kettle. She dragged the heavy kettle close to the basement door.

"Lizzie, help me," Eliza said.

Lizzie scurried out from the fort she'd built for herself under a table in the basement. "How?"

"We'll tip it together. Don't get wet." Together, they tipped the pot until the cloudy rinse water poured out into the garden. Lizzie squealed with pleasure and threw a handful of little flower buds into the stream of water.

"Look, Lizzie, you have your own river!" Eliza said.

Ma stood watching them. Eliza caught a smile playing on her mother's lips. When Ma saw Eliza's eyes on her, she threw her shawl over her shoulders. "It's time to go," she said. Now that the workday was over, Eliza could hear the fatigue in her mother's voice.

"Harriet!" It was Miss Charlotte standing at the parlor

window. "Before you leave, come up and see me."

"Of course, Miss Charlotte."

"And bring Eliza," Miss Charlotte added.

"That's not necessary," Ma protested. "She can wait down here with her sister."

"Nonsense! I insist," Miss Charlotte said. "Have Cook look after Lizzie. It's Eliza I want to talk to you about."

CHAPTER *Six*

"WE'LL BE RIGHT THERE," MA CALLED UP. TURNING TO ELIZA, Ma whispered fiercely, "What did you do?"

Eliza felt as though her feet had grown roots. "Nothing, Ma," she lied. What if Miss Charlotte told her mother about what had happened in the kitchen? Ma would never let Eliza out of her sight again.

After a quick scrub with a rag and some fresh water, Eliza followed her mother into the house. Eliza had never been inside Miss Charlotte's parlor before; she'd only glimpsed it through the windows from the garden. It was full of soft chairs and gleaming tables. There was a little porcelain clock on a marble-topped table. The walls were decorated with portraits of solemn men and women. A thick carpet with a pattern of red roses covered most of the polished wooden floors.

Her eyes taking in every detail of the room, Eliza made a marvelous discovery. Miss Charlotte had an upright piano tucked away in the corner. Eliza had never heard any piano music in the house; perhaps it was a new purchase. On closer look, she saw that the instrument was well used. There were indentations in the keys showing that someone played it frequently. The piano's surface was spotless—Miss Charlotte's servants dusted daily—but it had a forlorn look. Eliza's fingers itched to press the keys. She was sure she could learn to play if she had the chance. After all, if she could sing the notes, she should be able to plunk at the keys to make the same sounds. She glanced at Ma, who hadn't noticed the piano at all. Well, Ma wouldn't, would she? She knew nothing of Eliza's secret dream.

Miss Charlotte was sitting in a padded chair, so plush it just begged for Eliza to curl up in its arms and take a nap. But Miss Charlotte sat up straight, her back not touching the upholstery. Eliza reached out to stroke the fabric of the chair nearest to her. Without turning her head, Ma slapped her hand away.

"How are you, Harriet?" Miss Charlotte asked.

"Very well, thank you." Ma's answer was polite but not forthcoming.

"And how is Dred?"

"He is fine." Ma paused and then seemed to decide that courtesy required more from her. "He's still working for Mr. Hall."

"Ah, the lawyer who took your case."

Ma shot a glance at Eliza, then said, "Thanks to you, Miss Charlotte."

Eliza's thoughts jerked away from the comfortable

furniture. She stared at her ma, then at Miss Charlotte. They owed their lawyer to Miss Charlotte? What else had Ma kept from her?

"I never expected your case to take so long," Miss Charlotte said.

Ma shrugged, whether as an apology or because she was resigned to wait, Eliza wasn't sure.

"The court opens on the third Monday in April. Mr. Hall says we'll be one of the first cases heard. Soon it will be over."

An unfamiliar look flitted across Ma's face. After a moment, Eliza recognized the expression as hope.

"But in the meantime, you and the children have to stay in that dreadful place," Miss Charlotte said. "I've been worried about you being there."

"That's very kind, ma'am," Ma said, as she put an arm around Eliza's waist. "But so long as we're together, we'll be fine."

Miss Charlotte stood up and began walking about the room. She absentmindedly ran her hand along the top of the mantle, then examined her fingers for dust. She turned to face Ma. "I have a suggestion. My husband's aunt just came to live with us. She can be difficult to handle. But today Eliza's singing calmed her right away."

Eliza straightened up with a quick glance at her mother. What was Miss Charlotte after?

Ma's eyes narrowed. "That's very nice, but . . ."

"In addition to her singing, Eliza's manners are very good—she's a credit to you and Dred. I think Eliza's the perfect person to mind Aunt Sofia. And she can stay here, which would relieve your mind, I'm sure."

Eliza drew in a quick breath. She'd never dreamed of living in a house so grand. Taking care of Miss Sofia would be so much easier than doing laundry, day in, day out. She'd sleep on a proper bed and eat Cook's food and see her friend Sadie every day. Best of all, Ma wouldn't be watching her every move. Eliza stepped forward, nodding eagerly. She stopped short when she heard Ma, already deciding for her.

"Thank you for the offer, but Eliza will stay with her family."

"But, Ma," Eliza began. "I would like to . . ."

Ma shot her a warning look.

Eliza sighed. Trying to go against Ma was like trying to hold back the river in full flood; it couldn't be done.

Miss Charlotte's lips were pinched. After a few moments, she said, "If you change your mind, Harriet, I'd be glad to have her here."

"You've been very good to us," Ma admitted. "But Eliza is safer with us."

"I think she'd be safer here—but it's your decision."

Under her breath, Eliza muttered, "The decision should be mine."

Miss Charlotte picked up a cloth bag from a side table. Eliza hadn't noticed it before. "Eliza's growing clean out of her clothes, so I put aside a dress for her."

Eliza couldn't tear her eyes from the bag. A new dress.

If it hadn't been improper, she'd have shucked off her old tattered dress and put the new one on right there.

"That's kind, Miss Charlotte, but we can't accept." Then Ma glanced at Eliza's face and hesitated. For an instant Eliza thought she saw tears in Ma's eyes—but Ma never cried.

"Please." Eliza mouthed the word.

"Harriet, don't be proud," Miss Charlotte scolded. "You have to keep Eliza decent."

"Ma, I can't go out like this!" Eliza gestured to the ripped sleeve, now hanging onto her dress by only a few threads.

Finally Ma said, "I'll accept if you take the cost out of my pay."

"But it's a gift!" Miss Charlotte exclaimed.

"You've already done too much for us," Ma said stubbornly.

"Very well, I'll take it out of your wages," Miss Charlotte replied. Eliza smiled to herself. Ma didn't actually receive her wages. All the money went to the sheriff until their case was decided.

"Thank you," Ma said.

Miss Charlotte nodded. "You know I'm happy to help . . . so long as it stays between us."

Eliza's eyes darted from Miss Charlotte to her mother. The conversation had arrived somewhere Eliza didn't understand. Ma's face had closed up—Eliza would get no answers there.

"Yes, ma'am; thank you, ma'am." Ma hurried out of the parlor, towing Eliza behind her.

"Ma, you're hurting me," she complained.

"It's time to go home," Ma said, releasing Eliza's arm.

"It's not home, Ma," Eliza blurted out, unable to hide the bitterness she felt. "I hate that place. Even Miss Charlotte knows it's awful. She doesn't want me to live there."

Ma fixed Eliza with a stare. "Miss Charlotte has known about our living arrangements for months. It's only when she needs something that she decides to do anything about it."

"So?" Eliza countered. "She still offered." She held up the bundle. "And she gave me a dress."

"We don't need her charity," Ma insisted.

"You let her get us a lawyer!" Eliza shot back.

Ma ignored her. She collected Lizzie from the kitchen, then headed out to the garden. Eliza hurried after her.

"Ma, why won't you tell me the truth?" Eliza asked.

Ma started for the gate, but Eliza grabbed her sleeve. Lizzie clung to Ma's skirts. "These aren't matters for children." Ma jerked her arm away.

"I'm practically grown up, Ma."

Ma put her hands on her hips and scowled at Eliza. "Yes, you are. That's why we're suing Mrs. Emerson for your freedom."

"It's not just for me—it's for all of us!" Eliza cried.

"The older you get, the more danger you are in—don't you see that? Unless we get the court to say we're free people, we can't protect you. We work for no wages and live in that awful place so you and Lizzie don't have to be afraid like your pa and me."

"But I'm not afraid," Eliza answered. "I want to take the job."

Ma gritted her teeth. "All these years I've been telling you how dangerous the world is, you still haven't learned a thing. You are safe with us. Nowhere else."

"I'd be safer here," Eliza insisted. "No one would dare touch me if I lived here. Look at Sadie—she's not afraid."

"Sadie doesn't have any more sense than you. She could be sold at any time." Ma gripped Eliza's hand tightly. "Eliza, she's a slave. She's property. And Miss Charlotte can do whatever she wants with her."

"Miss Charlotte is a good person," Eliza said stubbornly. She glanced back at the house. Sadie was lighting the lamps in the parlor. Miss Charlotte sat in her chair sewing.

"Yes. But what if Miss Charlotte died? Her son's a no-good rascal. What would happen to Sadie, then?"

Eliza shivered. She knew that no slave would be safe if Mark Charless were in charge.

"We may live in a terrible place," Ma continued, "and we can't call our wages our own. But we also can't be sold. When the judge sets us free, no one will ever buy or sell us again."

"But . . ."

"Your pa and I know best. You are not going to work for Miss Charlotte. You're going to stop asking questions, act younger than your age, and stay close to us until the case is settled. Then we'll see."

"But . . ."

"That's final." Ma threw open the garden gate and stomped outside, dragging a protesting Lizzie with her. The gate slammed shut.

Eliza took a last look at the house with all its comforts. The garden smelled of fresh herbs. The aroma of Cook's bread drifted out of the kitchen like a blessing. Reluctantly, she turned her back and followed Ma into the gathering darkness.

CHAPTER *Seven*

Eliza's hands were shaking and her fingers couldn't seem to unlatch the gate. Finally she managed it and slipped through. Her new dress, in a bag slung over her shoulder, caught on the wooden gate. She tugged it hard, tears springing to her eyes, until it came free.

Pa was there in the alley, leaning against the wall, talking to the Charlesses' stable man. He was almost twice as big as Pa. Pa's grin faded when Ma pushed past him, Lizzie struggling to keep up.

"Harriet?" he called. "What's wrong?"

Eliza shut the garden gate behind her and walked slowly to Pa. He held out his arms, and she stepped into his big hug. Standing as tall as he did, she rested her head on his shoulder.

"What's wrong, gypsy girl?" he asked. Eliza had been born on a steamboat named *Gipsy* going north on the Mississippi River. Hearing Pa call her that always made her feel better. How could a gypsy girl not have adventures someday?

"Hi, Pa," she said, smiling in spite of her bad mood.

Pa saw the bandage on her hand. "Are you hurt?"

"It's just a cut."

"Let me see." She held out her hand, and he deftly removed the bandage and examined the wound. Pa had learned a lot about medicine when he had been Dr. Emerson's slave. "You cleaned it?"

She nodded. "Cook ran the pump water over it."

He began to rewrap the bandage. "That water's clean," he said. "This should heal fine."

"Pa, can I ask you a question?" She peered over Pa's shoulder to make sure Ma was out of earshot. She and Lizzie were waiting at the end of the alley, staying clear of the passing carriages.

"'Course you can."

"Before Dr. Emerson, who did you work for?" she asked.

His head jerked toward the Charlesses' house. "I think you already know the answer," he said slowly.

Eliza tilted her head to one side, the tufted end of her braid brushing against her shoulder. "Then it doesn't matter if you tell me all about it," she coaxed.

He hesitated. "It was long ago."

"Then why is it a secret?" she asked.

Pa shifted from one foot to another as though the ground weren't quite firm. "It's not. You just didn't have any reason to know."

"That's what Ma said," Eliza snapped. "But she's wrong. Why is Miss Charlotte helping us?"

"Shhh," he hissed, eyes darting up and down the alley. "That's family business, best not discussed where people might hear."

"According to Ma, best not discussed at all!"

"Ah," he said, looking toward Ma, who was tapping her foot while Lizzie tugged at her skirt. "So that's why your ma looks like thunder?"

Eliza nodded. "Miss Charlotte offered me a good job, but Ma said no."

"Then that's that," he said. Pa rarely went against Ma's wishes. "Let's go."

It took only a moment to catch up with Ma. Her expression was still troubled, and Pa touched her cheek. "Home?" Pa asked.

"Do we have to?" Eliza pleaded. "It's Saturday and there's so much to see."

Pa asked Ma, "Harriet, are you too tired?"

"A walk will do us good," Ma answered after a moment. "Let's go to the Cathedral." Pa held out his arm, and Ma threaded her arm through his.

"We can see Jack," Eliza said.

"And Punch and Judy," Lizzie chimed in.

Saturday was the best day to wander the city, but Eliza really wanted to postpone the moment when the doors clanged shut behind them for the night. If only Ma would be reasonable, Eliza would never have to stay there again.

Pa picked up Lizzie and put her on his shoulders. Before they had traveled half a block, Pa had Lizzie giggling. The happy sound was better than any tonic from a doctor. Soon Eliza was smiling, and even Ma's mood improved. Ma reached out and squeezed Eliza's hand. Eliza squeezed back. What would she do without Ma? And Lizzie and Pa? If she worked for Miss Charlotte, she wouldn't see them every day. Eliza sighed. Since Ma had already decided for her, Eliza needn't worry about it.

She swung her arms and lengthened her stride. She winced when she heard the fabric under her arms tear. *At least I have a new dress*, she thought, feeling the package bounce on her back.

Even though the city streets were wide, they were crowded on a Saturday when most folks were finished with work. Food sellers were offering crackling bits of sausage and meat pies. They jostled for space with stalls filled with pots, pans, and pretty bolts of cloth. The goods for sale seemed endless. Pa stopped in front of one stall and admired a bonnet made of a yellow cloth with tiny blue flowers. "You'd look awfully nice wearing one of those," he said to Ma.

"It's too young for me," Ma disagreed. "But the yellow would suit Eliza just fine."

Eliza imagined wearing the bonnet to church the next day. She'd tie the ribbons under her chin and hope Wilson would think it was pretty. "Can I try it on?" she asked.

Ma's smile dried up and she hurried Eliza down the street. "We can't afford to buy anything," she whispered fiercely. "And that man"—she jerked her head back to the bonnet seller—"he won't want the likes of us touching his wares."

Feeling very daring, Eliza said, "Ma, if I worked for Miss Charlotte, I could use my wages to buy a bonnet. And something nice for Lizzie too."

"We don't need pretty things."

Eliza stared down at the ground. She'd made Ma angry again.

In a gentler voice, Ma said, "Eliza, let's just enjoy the afternoon." She took Eliza's hand. "Stay close."

"Yes, Ma."

They turned onto Elm Street to see the Cathedral looming over the small square. There was a grassy park in front of the church filled with families. Lizzie squealed when she saw the wooden puppet theater. Punch the puppet was smacking Judy on the head. "Pa, let's go!" Lizzie said, urging him forward.

"Can I visit Jack?" Eliza asked.

"Don't go too far," Ma said, but she was watching Pa and Lizzie, a hint of a smile on her lips.

Jack was an old friend who had a cart on the corner. A wizened black man, he was missing half his teeth, but that didn't stop him from always having a ready smile for Eliza. His cart was filled with ribbons, combs, tiny mirrors— anything to attract the ladies. Eliza hurried over to see what was new.

"Hello, Miss Eliza," Jack greeted her.

"Hi, Jack," she responded. She stared at a new addition to the cart: a flat circular stone set in a wheel. "What's that?" she asked.

"I've started sharpening knives and scissors," Jack replied.

"I'm going to make a pretty penny with this, let me tell you."
Jack patted the wheel. "And best of all, it comes with a song."

Eliza stood at attention. "A song?"

He began to sing:

Any knives or scissors to grind?
Bring me knives or scissors to grind.
I will make them fine as new.
Just the way you want me to.

Eliza waited until she knew the tune and then joined in.
People walking by stopped to listen. When they were done, a
white woman offered Eliza a penny.

"Give it back." Ma's voice filled Eliza's ear. She hadn't
even realized Ma was there. "No daughter of mine will sing
for money. Singing is for church."

Eliza felt her face burning as she handed the coin back to
the woman.

"Aw, Mrs. Scott, Eliza's singing never did no harm," Jack
said in his soothing voice.

Eliza wasn't listening—her embarrassment felt like water
closing over her head; she couldn't breathe. When would Ma
just let her be?

Eliza didn't speak while Ma collected everyone to head
home. Lizzie was busy chattering with Pa as Ma and Eliza
walked in stony silence. When Chestnut Street started to
climb, Eliza knew they were almost at the St. Louis County

Jail. Her steps slowed as though the hill were even steeper than it was.

"Don't dawdle," Ma called over her shoulder.

Eliza made a face at her mother's back. She could never bring herself to think of the jail as home, even though they slept there every night. It was all Mrs. Emerson's fault. Most freedom litigants lived and worked in the city, waiting for their case to be decided. But Mrs. Emerson was so furious about their lawsuit, she insisted that the sheriff keep the Scott family in the jailhouse. Every morning Ma and Pa left the jail to work, but they had to report back each night. The sheriff held their pay and even charged them for room and board. So the respectable Scotts had to live in the same building with murderers and thieves. They were the only freedom litigants living in the jail now, and Lizzie and Eliza were the only children.

The sight of the jailhouse made Eliza's stomach ache. The building was three stories high, plain, and square. Eliza had never been on the upper stories where the real criminals were kept. In front there was an entry hall tacked on. Going through the entryway was like a tunnel into hell. There was a small courtyard for exercise, but no one ever used it. Eliza had heard that they used to hang men there, and to her the courtyard smelled of suffering.

They lived on the ground floor with a few prisoners who had short sentences, called trustees. Ma and the girls were in one cell while Pa slept in another cell with three other men.

The only good thing you could say about the jail was that the Scotts had a roof over their heads. Otherwise, it was a place where hope and happiness went to waste away.

As they neared the entrance, they couldn't miss the sound of a crowd gathered at the corner. There were men and women who'd had too much to drink, a few ordinary people on their way to somewhere else, as well as the usual batch of boys who had no better place to go. Eliza couldn't make out any words amongst all the cursing and shouting. Ma looked a sharp question at Pa. He handed Lizzie to Ma. "Wait here. I'll find out what's happening."

"Maybe it's a jail break," Eliza said excitedly.

"Don't even think that," Ma scolded. "The prisoners aren't like us—they're bad people."

Pa pushed through the crowd to see a young black girl land hard on the cobblestones right at his feet. Wheeling his arms to keep his balance, he managed not to step on her. A big white man barreled after her. The girl's hair was pulled out of its braids and hung tangled in front of her face. Her dress was torn at the shoulder and the waist. She scrambled to her feet to run away, but her pursuer grabbed her arm and twisted it behind her. She cried out with pain. The crowd backed away, and only then did Eliza see her face.

"Ma! It's Lucy!" Eliza shouted. A quick look at Ma's stricken face, and Eliza knew Ma had recognized the girl from the old days at the river. Lucy and Eliza had been friends until Lucy had been sent to the block.

Pa plucked Lizzie from Ma's arms and held her against his chest. "She's a fugitive now," he said for Ma's ears.

"Let me see her!" A heavyset white man wearing a dark suit, cigar in his hand, shoved past Eliza to look at Lucy. "This one's cost me a heap of trouble." He grabbed her chin, forcing her to look at him. Eliza gasped when she saw Lucy's eyes, sunken deep in her face. Back when Eliza knew her, Lucy had been such a pretty girl.

"It's Reuben Bartlett," Pa said under his breath, but Eliza could just make out the words.

"Lucy," the man said in a louder voice. He slapped her face until she opened her eyes.

"Stop hitting her!" Eliza cried.

Bartlett's eyes zipped over to Eliza faster than a dragonfly on the Mississippi. And he dismissed her just as quickly. Eliza started forward, but her mother's hand on her shoulder jerked Eliza back.

"Stay still," Ma hissed. "Bartlett's the worst slave catcher in the country."

Bartlett slapped Lucy again. "Wake up! Do you know where you are?"

Lucy mumbled something. Eliza thought she might have said, "The jail?"

He nodded. "You'll be locked up here until my boat can take you back to Louisiana. If you run again, I'll kill you." With a nod to his man, he said, "Let her go."

The man holding Lucy let her fall to the ground. She was

as limp as a wet cloth, but the thud she made striking the cobblestones turned Eliza's stomach. Bartlett stared down at her for a moment, and the look on his face was the purest mean Eliza had ever witnessed. His right foot moved back, ready to kick Lucy in the belly.

"No!" Without thinking, Eliza pulled out of Ma's grasp. She threw herself over Lucy's body and braced herself.

"Eliza!" Ma's cry sounded above her head.

Eliza's eyes were fixed on the toe of Bartlett's boot swinging toward her head.

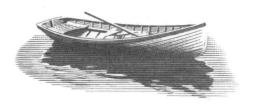

CHAPTER *Eight*

S UDDENLY BARTLETT WAS HAULED BACKWARDS. "BARTLETT, don't you dare kick that girl!" a man shouted. Bartlett's foot stopped in midair. Eliza's stomach stayed clenched, but she let herself breathe again. It was Mr. Martin, the man in charge of the jail. He was a young man but confident, with his uniform and his authority.

"Stay out of this, Martin. This has nothing to do with you!" Bartlett snarled.

"I can't stop you from abusing the slaves you catch," Mr. Martin spat. "But I won't let you touch this girl. She's under my protection."

Pa's hands were patting Eliza all over to make sure there were no injuries.

"Pa, I'm sorry," she whispered.

"Hush," he murmured. Eliza saw how he kept his body between her and Bartlett.

"She was interfering with the lawful capture of a fugitive,"

Bartlett announced loudly, wanting the crowd to hear.

"She's a little girl, Bartlett!" Mr. Martin declared. "If you want this jail to continue to hold your fugitives, you'll go now."

"What about her?" Bartlett jabbed his finger at Lucy lying prone on the ground.

"I'll take charge of her."

Bartlett took a final puff of his cigar and dropped it to the ground. "Her name's Lucy Jones, and I've been chasing her for three days. Make sure she stays put until I collect my bounty."

"My jail is secure. She'll be here," Mr. Martin said. "Of course, I'll charge you for her keep—and any medical attention I decide she needs."

Bartlett puffed up and started to protest.

"You know the rules," Martin reminded him. "If you didn't beat them so badly, you'd save money on the doctor's bills."

Bartlett started to chuckle. "Now, that wouldn't be any fun at all." He gestured to his man to come with him, and they pushed their way through the crowd.

Pa held Eliza close to him while Ma clutched Lizzie to her breast. Mr. Martin directed his bailiff to bring Lucy inside. He came over to the Scotts. "Is Eliza hurt?"

"I'm fine," Eliza said, her forehead pressed against Pa's cheek.

"Dred, take Eliza inside," Mr. Martin ordered. He drew close so only Pa and Eliza could hear. "What were you thinking, tangling with Bartlett?"

"It was my fault," Eliza mumbled.

"It certainly was, young lady," Mr. Martin scolded. "Dred, I like you and your family. Take my advice and don't get in Bartlett's way again." He looked around at the crowd of curious gawkers. "Clear off, everyone—there's nothing more to see!"

Ma was trembling. With her free hand, she touched Eliza's face, gentle as a feather. But her words hit Eliza like a hammer. "He could have beaten you to death right here in front of us. In front of your little sister." Lizzie whimpered.

Her voice catching on a sob, Eliza said, "I'm sorry, Ma."

"You should be. You'd throw away everything for a girl we hardly know?" Ma asked fiercely. "Do you want to end up like her?"

"Lucy's a slave," Eliza insisted. "I'm free. You always say so."

"As if that matters to a slave catcher like Bartlett!" Ma spat out his name like it was a burning ember on her tongue. "If it hadn't been for Mr. Martin, you could have been killed and we couldn't have lifted a finger to stop it without being killed ourselves. Then who would take care of Lizzie?"

Tears streaming down her face, Eliza cried, "I said I was sorry."

"You're always sorry, but you never learn," Ma reprimanded her. She turned her back on Eliza and Pa and brought Lizzie inside. Eliza knew she would go straight to the kitchen to start dinner without resting even for an instant.

Pa and Eliza lingered outside. "We'll give your ma a few minutes to calm down," he said.

"She was so mad," Eliza whispered.

"She was scared. So was I." He put his arm around Eliza's shoulders.

Eliza leaned against him for a minute, then turned to face him. "Pa, what will happen to Lucy?"

"Her owner will probably beat her or keep her in chains. If she's lucky, he'll sell her." He squeezed Eliza's hand. "Forget about Lucy. We can't do anything to help her now." Pa handed Eliza her bundled dress. She didn't remember dropping it. "Put this away and then come help with dinner."

Eliza walked slowly to the cell she shared with Ma and Lizzie. It had three straw beds and a chamber pot. A battered chest in the corner held their few belongings. She sat on her bed, turning the package over in her hands. Pa had told her there was nothing they could do to help Lucy, so she might as well look at her new dress. She opened the paper.

"Oh . . ." she exclaimed quietly. The dress was dark green, not slave blue. Apparently Miss Charlotte didn't think of Eliza as a slave. Maybe that was why she was helping with their lawsuit. Pa had a lot of explaining to do the next time she could get him alone. In the meantime, she held the dress to her shoulders. The green would flatter her skin, Eliza was sure of it. And the hem fell to the tops of her boots. The colors were the same as Wilson's ship. Maybe he would come to church and see her wearing it. She imagined his wide smile, eyes bright with admiration for her. But then the memory of

Lucy's body, bloody and bruised on the ground, elbowed the pleasant daydream out of her head.

Eliza pulled the dress away from her body. What kind of Christian girl was she to be thinking about courting when Lucy was suffering? Pa said there was nothing to do, but Eliza knew that wasn't true. She could visit Lucy and bring her a blanket. Maybe she could sneak some extra food to her? Anything to let Lucy know that she wasn't alone.

Her eyes went to the ceiling. The female prisoners were housed on the second floor. Eliza had never been up there. She knew the cells were locked, but the guards were reserved for the top floor where all the male criminals were housed. It would be easy to visit Lucy—especially now that Ma and Pa were busy with other tasks. She knew Ma wouldn't soon forgive Eliza if she found out where she'd gone, but helping Lucy was more important.

Before she could change her mind, Eliza grabbed one of her cotton blankets. Lucy would prefer it to the buffalo hide the jail would have given her. She took one of Ma's precious candles and lit it with a flint. She checked the hallway outside their cell—there was no one to see her. She slipped out of the cell, the metal door clanging behind her. She hated that noise—but at least the doors were never locked for the Scotts. They were free to come and go from their cells as they pleased.

Avoiding the common room where Ma was cooking, Eliza headed up the stairway to the second story. She assumed that the cells were arranged the same way as they were on the ground floor.

The hall was narrow with a scuffed and dented wooden floor. There were twelve cell doors in a row. A single lamp at the far end of the hallway was the only light. A draft of chilly air blew through the hall; Eliza cupped her hand around the candle flame to keep it from going out.

Eliza crept up to the first cell door and peered in. An older woman, not Lucy, was lying on the straw. She stared at Eliza but didn't say a word. The cells up here were smaller than the one Eliza slept in. She moved on. Her trembling hand made the candlelight jump and play on the ceiling. The next cell was empty. At the third, she heard Lucy's moans before she saw her slumped on the floor, leaning against the wall.

"Lucy," Eliza whispered.

There was no response, and Eliza wondered if she was asleep. "Lucy!" she called again, a little louder.

Lucy's eyes opened a crack, then wider when she saw Eliza.

"Remember me?" She held the candle to her face so Lucy could recognize her. "I'm Eliza from down by the river."

"Are you running away too?" Lucy's voice sounded far away. "Don't go near the river. There's nowhere to hide. They'll catch you."

"No, I'm not running," Eliza answered softly. "Are you all right? I saw that man beat you."

Lucy's head tilted forward like she had fallen asleep. "That was nothing. My master beat me all the time. For no reason at all." Her voice faltered and Eliza leaned in to hear her better.

"No wonder you ran," Eliza said.

"I'd've done it months ago, but his men were always watching," Lucy explained. "But then the master went to Alabama for business. When he came back, he was sick. Real sick. Soon everyone was sick. That was my chance." She struggled to lift her head and squinted in the dim light.

"Why'd you come back here?" Eliza asked, thinking this was the first place a slave catcher would look for Lucy.

"Where else could I go? I have friends here. I was trying to get to the shantytown when they found me. I ran but they caught me and brought me here." She buried her face in her hands. "Now they'll hang me."

"My pa said they'll bring you back to your master."

"I'm better off dead." Eliza could barely make out her muffled words.

"You said he was sick. Maybe he's dead?" Eliza said hopefully.

Lucy was silent. Eliza stared at her, feeling helpless. If Ma wasn't so careful all the time, Eliza might be in Lucy's place. What was it Reverend Meachum said? "There but for the grace of God go I." God's grace and Ma's eagle eye kept Eliza safe.

"I brought you a blanket," Eliza said finally, shoving it through the bars of the door.

"I remember you now. Eliza. Eliza Scott." Lucy edged over to the door and pulled the blanket around her shoulders. "It was you, wasn't it, who got between me and Bartlett?"

Eliza nodded.

"You shouldn't have done that. Now he'll be after you

too." Suddenly Lucy vomited all over herself. She curled up like a baby, helpless in her own sick.

"Lucy, are you all right?" Eliza cried. "Lucy!" She reached through the bars and tugged on Lucy's hand, but she didn't wake up.

The woman in the first cell roused herself long enough to press her face against the cell door and complain. "Stop that caterwauling. I'm trying to sleep!"

"She's sick," Eliza said. "She won't wake up."

"She's better off asleep. Let her be," the prisoner said.

"No! She's my friend, and I'm going to help her." She'd find Mrs. Martin. The jailer's wife was also the jail's nurse. Eliza blew out her candle and ran for the stairs. At the top step, she hesitated for an instant. If she fetched Mrs. Martin, Ma was sure to find out where Eliza had dared to go. She gave herself a little shake. What was another argument with Ma weighed against Lucy's life?

She ran down the stairs. Avoiding the kitchen, she was lucky to find Mrs. Martin in the pantry counting sacks of rice. She was older than her husband with pale skin and hair as yellow and fine as corn silk.

"Lucy Jones needs a doctor!" Eliza blurted out.

"What do you know about Lucy?" Her blue eyes sharpening with suspicion, Mrs. Martin declared, "You know you're not allowed upstairs!"

Speaking as calmly as she could, Eliza replied, "Lucy told me that everyone is sick at her old place. A bad sickness. I think she brought it here. She needs help."

The blood drained from Mrs. Martin's face. A jail was a terrible place for illness—before long everyone would have it. "I'll have a look at her," she said.

"Yes, ma'am." Eliza bobbed her head. "Please be quick."

Mrs. Martin put aside the rice and went upstairs. Eliza sat on the bottom stair and waited. She leaned her elbows on her knees to keep her legs from shaking. After a few minutes, Mrs. Martin came hurrying down. Eliza leaped to her feet. "Well?" she asked.

"I'm sending for the doctor," Mrs. Martin told her. "Now promise me you won't go upstairs."

"I won't," Eliza assured her. "Hurry, please!"

Even as Mrs. Martin rushed away, her steps seemed heavy. Eliza gazed up the stairway. She couldn't go back, but that didn't stop her from praying. "Please, God, don't let Lucy die."

CHAPTER *Nine*

"ELIZA, STOKE UP THE FIRE IN THE OVEN, THEN SET THE TABLE," Ma instructed with a no-nonsense look in her eye. Ma didn't know about Eliza's visit to Lucy yet, but it was only a matter of time before Mrs. Martin returned with the doctor and told Ma everything.

"Yes, Ma," Eliza answered quickly.

The freedom litigants and the trustees had a common room for cooking and eating. Eliza found the room depressing. It was dingy, with low ceilings, and it smelled of too many meals and not enough soap. Besides the Scotts, there were only a few trustees, prisoners who weren't dangerous and had special privileges like Ma's helper, Mrs. George. She was an older white woman who had almost completed her sentence for thieving. Together they prepared dinner.

Eliza quietly brought in the wooden bowls from the back cupboard and set them carefully with metal spoons around the battered wooden table. She had done this chore a hundred times, but today her hands were clumsy. A bowl slipped from her hands and clattered to the floor. Ma jumped at the noise in the near-silent room.

A gurgle of laughter from the hall had Ma and Eliza turning to the door. The prison tomcat scurried in and hid under a table. Lizzie came chasing after him. Pa brought up the rear.

"Lizzie, be nice to the kitty," Eliza said. "Maybe he doesn't want to be chased." *Like Lucy*, she thought. *And all the other fugitives.*

"Eliza, let her play," Pa said. "She doesn't understand what happened outside today."

"I wish I didn't," Eliza murmured.

"Come sit with me," Pa said. He patted a spot on the wooden bench against the wall farthest from the kitchen. They sat quietly watching Ma and Mrs. George prepare dinner. Pa's hand curled around Eliza's.

Pa broke the silence first. "What's worrying you, gypsy girl?"

Eliza's fear for Lucy was squeezing her stomach and making her feel ill, but she couldn't tell Pa. He'd be sure to ask how Eliza knew Lucy was sick. But there were other things she could talk to Pa about, especially while Ma was busy elsewhere.

"Miss Charlotte's family used to own you," she began. "I didn't even know you knew her!"

"I've known Miss Charlotte all my life. I minded her when she was a babe." As though Ma knew Pa was telling secrets, she gave them a sharp look before she returned her attention to a pot bubbling on the stove.

Eliza couldn't imagine a world where her pa was in charge of a grand lady like Miss Charlotte. "Were you born in Virginia?"

"So they tell me," he said with a shrug.

"Who were your parents?" Eliza asked.

"I never knew." There was no emotion in his voice. For Pa, being an orphan was just how things were. "Miss Charlotte's family was the only one I ever had."

"Your owners can't be your family," Eliza said decisively. "We're your family."

He stroked her hand. "Most colored folk in this country don't get to keep their family. It's why your ma and I are fighting this law case so hard—so we can keep you close."

Eliza thought about that. Lucy had had no one to care about her, and look how she ended up. "I guess I'm pretty lucky," she admitted.

"Your ma always watches over you," Pa reminded her.

"Let's not talk about Ma," Eliza said sourly, and Pa chuckled. "What did you do for Miss Charlotte's family?"

"I'm not big enough to be much good in the fields, so I mainly looked after the children. That's when I took care of Miss Charlotte. But the master wasn't good with money. He had to sell a lot of us, including my wife, to pay his debts."

Eliza turned to see his face. Pa's eyes were staring, unfocused, as though he was looking deep into his memories.

"Your wife?" she cried, loudly enough that Ma shot her a

suspicious look. "Does that mean you're not married to Ma?" Eliza whispered.

"No, no." Pa was quick to reassure her. "Master Peter let me and Phillis marry, but only 'until death or distance did us part.' When Phillis was sold, our marriage was over too. I never saw her again."

Eliza felt the strength of Pa's grip on her hand. He and Ma must worry that Eliza or Lizzie might vanish one day like Phillis had.

"But you aren't married to Ma like that?"

He shook his head. "We're married tight as tight. So don't you worry." He patted her shoulder. Eliza noticed that Ma's helper, Mrs. George, had told a joke that made Ma laugh. Lizzie had finally cornered the cat, and it was curled up on her lap, purring loudly. Eliza hated it when the common room felt homey. She didn't ever want it to be a place where she felt comfortable.

Pa went on, "We came to St. Louis, and Miss Charlotte grew up. She married Mr. Charless." He began to laugh. "No one thought we'd ever see the day when the master would let his little girl marry an abolitionist. But Miss Charlotte liked him, and Charless was a rich man. He agreed to let her keep the slaves she had but not to buy any more."

Eliza's head was beginning to ache. How could Miss Charlotte, who owned dozens of slaves, marry an abolitionist? And why should she help Pa with his legal case? And why was it a secret?

"The next year the master sold me to Dr. Emerson. The

doctor brought me to the territories, where I met your ma."

Eliza knew that those territories were north of Missouri and that the U.S. government said there was no slavery there. The so-called Missouri Compromise was the reason for their law case.

Eliza couldn't wait any longer. "Pa, why is a slave owner helping us get free?"

"She's a kind lady."

"No one is that kind," Eliza protested.

Pa lifted his shoulders in a shrug. "I asked her to sign a bond when we filed our case. She said yes, but then did even more. She hired Mr. Hall to be our lawyer. But it would embarrass Miss Charlotte if people knew. Her friends would think she'd followed her husband's politics."

Ma beckoned them to come get their food. Eliza jumped to her feet, her stomach making a rumbling noise. She gave Pa her hand.

"These old bones are getting stiff," he complained.

"You're not old," she said. "I'll get Lizzie washed up."

As Eliza and Lizzie pumped water into the washbasin by the back door, Mrs. Martin passed them on her way to the stairs. A doctor in a black coat followed behind. Eliza watched them go, wondering and worrying.

"Eliza! Stop!" Lizzie shouted.

Startled, Eliza looked down to see the water overflowing the basin. "Sorry, Lizzie."

At dinner, Eliza and Lizzie lined up behind the trustees and their parents to pile their plates high with beans and early collard greens flavored with some pork back fat. As she ate, Eliza kept an eye on the door, but there was no sign of the doctor. When Ma's back was turned, Eliza licked her bowl clean. Lizzie gave the leftover sauce in her bowl to the tomcat.

After dinner, Eliza did the washing up with Lizzie's help. Ma and Pa sat at the table talking with Mrs. George. Their faces were somber, and Eliza guessed they were discussing Lucy.

"Dred," Mrs. Martin interrupted, "will you come to the infirmary?"

Ma's and Pa's eyes met. The biscuits in Eliza's stomach turned to rocks. What had the doctor said? Was Lucy in the infirmary now? And why Pa?

"I'll be glad to," Pa replied. Pa handed Eliza his empty bowl and spoon to put in the soapy water and disappeared down the hall with Mrs. Martin.

Usually Ma preened a bit when Pa was asked for his medical advice, as though it made her family more important. But tonight she looked worried.

"Why does she need Dred?" Mrs. George asked.

Ma's gaze was fixed on the door and she didn't answer.

"Ma, what's happening?" Eliza asked.

"Nothing for you to concern yourself with."

Her lips pressed together to keep from arguing with Ma, Eliza scrubbed the pots hard enough to make them shine.

A short time later Pa came back. He had to steady himself on the end of the table. Ma put her hand over his. "What is it, Dred?" she asked.

He whispered in her ear, and Ma's body went still. Desperate to know what was happening, Eliza collected the remaining spoons and knives, but Pa stopped whispering when Eliza neared them.

"Take Lizzie and get ready for bed, Eliza," he told her.

"But I'm not done with the dishes," she protested. *And I deserve to know!* she thought.

"Don't argue with me, young lady!" Pa said sharply.

"Take Lizzie and don't leave the cell," Ma added.

Eliza grabbed Lizzie's hand and headed out. She walked slowly, hoping her parents would let something slip, but they were watching and waiting for them to go. Was Lucy worse? Was Lucy dead? Was it something else altogether?

When they reached the hall, Lizzie tugged on Eliza's arm. "Ma sounded scared," Lizzie said.

"I'm sure everything is all right." Eliza tried to sound reassuring.

"Eliza, you sound scared too."

CHAPTER *Ten*

Back in their cell, Eliza helped her sister into a nightdress but kept her own clothes on. She arranged Lizzie's faded blanket on the straw bed. Ma had collected dozens of blankets to keep them warm. Even this past winter when the damp had seeped through the walls and icicles formed inside the window, they hadn't been cold.

Ma did her best to make the cell feel like home, but Eliza always felt like the walls were closing in on her—maybe because every wall was the same whitewashed color. Ma kept the narrow room spotless and washed the stone floor every week. But every night Eliza breathed through her mouth to avoid the smell of jail that just never went away.

"Sing me a song," Lizzie demanded as she crawled under the blanket.

"Just one and you have to close your eyes," Eliza said. Lizzie squeezed her eyes shut. Eliza sang one of her own tunes.

I was born on the Mississippi
On a night it was raising Cain.
And every time I think of my ma
I think of the pouring rain.

"Ma won't let you say 'Cain,'" Lizzie mumbled.

"Go to sleep," Eliza said. When Lizzie finally fell asleep, Eliza left the candle burning in its holder and slipped out of the cell. She refused to let her parents protect her from bad news. Eliza would find out what was going on.

She hurried to the common room. The door was closed, so she crouched down and put her ear to the crack next to the floor.

"That poor girl." Eliza heard Mrs. Martin's voice on the other side of the door.

Mrs. George answered, "As if she didn't have troubles enough."

Mrs. Martin's whisper was just barely audible to Eliza. "I'm not supposed to say anything," she began, in that tone of voice that meant she was going to tell Mrs. George everything. "The doctor doesn't want to cause a panic, but he thinks it's . . ." There was a pause as if the word was too awful to say. "Cholera."

"Cholera!"

Eliza caught her breath. Lucy had cholera? That was even worse than Eliza had imagined. Cholera was a killer. No one knew what caused it or what cured it either. If cholera was in the jail, they were all in deadly danger.

"We're keeping it quiet," Mrs. Martin went on. "The doctor could be wrong."

"Is the girl vomiting?" Mrs. George asked. "Is her stool watery? Does she have cramps?"

"All those things," Mrs. Martin said sadly.

"Wretched girl!" Mrs. George exclaimed. "She'll give it to all of us!"

Eliza nearly fell over, she was so indignant. It wasn't Lucy's fault she was sick!

"You can't blame her," protested Mrs. Martin, speaking the words Eliza wanted to say. "For now, she'll stay in the infirmary. Harriet and Dred Scott are watching her. Dred's owner was a doctor, and Dred's good with sick folks."

Eliza was frozen to the spot. Her pity for Lucy was mixed now with fear for herself and her family. What was Pa thinking?

"What if the sickness spreads?" Mrs. George asked. "It won't be safe here."

"That is up to my husband," Mrs. Martin replied. "He'll do everything possible to keep everyone safe."

The women moved out of earshot. That was all right with Eliza; she had plenty to think about. She scurried back to her cell. Lizzie was snoring on the floor. Eliza climbed into bed and held her sister tightly. Cholera! Ma had told her about it. A man would be hale and hearty one day and dead the next. It was painful and disgusting—with the sick coming out of the patient from both ends. And since they didn't know what caused it, how would Pa keep from getting ill himself?

Eliza heard Ma's footsteps in the hall coming toward their cell. She snuffed out the candle and pulled the blanket up to her nose before the candle smoke hit the air.

Eliza willed her body to be as still as a corpse. To her surprise, Ma didn't get ready for bed. Instead she rummaged in their small chest until she found what she was looking for. A moment later the smell of camphor filled the small cell. It was a particularly nasty medicine that Ma would apply to Eliza's skin when she had a rash or a bug bite.

Eliza opened her eyes to watch Ma pull out a little brush and begin painting the cell bars with the medicine.

"What are you doing, Ma?" Eliza asked, yawning as if she had been awakened.

If Ma was startled, she didn't show it. She kept brushing, up and down and around the bars. "Never you mind, Eliza. Go back to sleep."

Eliza closed her eyes, pretending to sleep. Then Ma put on her nightdress and got into bed. For a long time, Eliza heard a faint murmuring. Ma was praying.

Eliza wanted to sit up and say, *Praying won't help us if Pa puts himself in cholera's way.* But she held her tongue and bided her time. As soon as Ma fell asleep, Eliza was going to find Pa in the infirmary and tell him exactly what she thought.

The "infirmary" wasn't much different from Eliza's cell except that it was bigger and had four cots with proper sheets on them. The room was at the end of the hall, farthest from the noise of the street. A thick curtain hung in the doorway.

It must be almost midnight by now. The jail was quiet except for Lucy's moans. Eliza slid quietly up to the cell door and pulled the curtain aside. The room was ablaze with light from two lanterns. Pa sat on a wooden stool next to the bed, and he was washing Lucy's face with a small towel. When he moved, his shadow flitted wildly across the white walls.

Lucy started to vomit. Pa grabbed a bucket. Lucy threw up just a little thick liquid—she must not have anything left in her stomach. Eliza's stomach roiled too, and she tasted a little sick in her mouth. She must have made a sound because Pa glanced behind him. His eyes went wide when he saw Eliza.

"What are you doing here?" he shouted. "Get out!"

"Pa, I need to talk to you," Eliza said, and started to walk into the infirmary.

"For God's sake, Eliza, stay away."

"If it's not safe for me, then it's not safe for you."

Suddenly Eliza's arm was grabbed so hard it almost jerked out of the socket. Her mother dragged Eliza out the door.

"Ma, you're hurting me."

"What are you doing here?" Ma demanded.

"I wanted to tell Pa that he shouldn't nurse Lucy. Cholera is too dangerous."

She stared defiantly, daring Ma to lie.

Ma loosened her hold. "How do you know about the cholera?"

"Why didn't you tell me?" Eliza shot back.

"You're a child. Your pa and I will decide what you need to know." She pointed down the hall, and Eliza marched back to the cell, with her mother right behind her. Ma pushed Eliza in and carefully closed the door. Eliza frowned as Ma pulled a key from her pocket and locked the door.

"But we never lock the door!" Eliza protested.

"We do tonight," her mother snapped. "You are going to stay put until morning. We don't have time to worry about you."

"Ma!" Eliza rattled the cell door. The smell of camphor set her eyes to watering. "Ma, let me out." The fading sound of her mother's footsteps was her only answer.

CHAPTER *Eleven*

A CLANG OF METAL ON METAL WOKE ELIZA WITH A START. PA
stood in the cell's open doorway looking as though he hadn't
slept at all. Lizzie was curled up against Eliza's back, but Ma
was nowhere to be seen.

"Good morning, Eliza," Pa said.

"Where's Ma?" she asked. Moving gingerly away from
Lizzie, Eliza got to her feet, her back stiff from the thin straw
bed. She peered behind Pa in the dim light. "She locked me
in!"

"Now, Eliza, your ma only did what I would have done,"
her father warned. "You should never have been in the
infirmary."

"You shouldn't be there either," Eliza cried. "What will
happen to all of us if you get cholera?"

"I raised you better than that." She could see the
disappointment in his face. "Lucy needs my help."

Eliza couldn't meet his eyes. She'd been thinking of herself, not poor Lucy. "How is she?"

"She's resting." He pulled her into his gentle hug. "I understand that you're worried, but I'll be careful."

"You and Ma yelled at me when I tried to help Lucy."

"I know the risks and I made a choice to help her. But you always leap first, then think about the consequences. You're not scared enough."

"Of what?" Eliza asked, confused.

"Everything. No matter how many times we warn you about running off by yourself, getting in a slave catcher's way, going to the second floor when you aren't supposed to, sneaking into the infirmary—you do it anyway."

"The second floor?" Eliza asked. She didn't think Pa knew about that.

He tilted her chin up with one finger. "I found your blanket wrapped around Lucy. Who else could have given it to her?"

"I didn't know she was sick." Eliza grabbed his hand; it was raw from scrubbing. "What about you? How will you keep from getting ill?"

"I'm fine," he said with a heavy sigh. "Dr. Emerson taught me to scrub my hands after I'm with a sick patient."

"Everyone says there's no cure for cholera," Eliza said in a small voice.

"Dr. Emerson had some good luck pulling his patients through by giving them lots of clean, boiled water. That's why Lucy's eyes were so dark—there's no water left in her body."

"Will she live?" Eliza held her breath waiting for the answer.

He rubbed the bridge of his nose. "I hope so. But she's pretty sick. I don't know how she managed to run all the way to St. Louis." He gave her a quick hug. "That's enough said about things we can't change. Mrs. Martin is going to look after Lucy while we go to church." At that moment, Lizzie rolled over and stretched. "I'll take care of Lizzie," Pa said. "Go wash up. And fix those braids. You have to look your best on the Lord's Day."

When Eliza returned, Ma was in the cell, neatly dressed as usual. Their eyes met and there was an awkward silence. After Pa nudged Eliza, she burst into an apology. "I'm sorry for sneaking out last night. I was just worried about everyone."

The sternness on Ma's face softened. "Your big heart is going to get you into trouble someday."

"I'll do better," Eliza promised, and in that moment she meant it.

The heavy doors shut behind them as they walked out into the bright sun. Eliza felt lighter, as if the jail itself had been weighing her down. Hurrying out in front of her parents, she decided she couldn't do Lucy any good by being sad. And there was so much to look forward to today. First, there was no laundry. Second, Eliza would be singing the solo with the choir. Third, she was wearing a new dress. Best of all, fourth and finally, she got to go to school that afternoon.

The church was only a few blocks away from the jailhouse, and Eliza made the most of every step. Glancing back, she saw Lizzie perched on Pa's back, and his arm was threaded through Ma's—just like they were ordinary free people going to church on a Sunday morning.

"Don't get too far ahead," her mother scolded, but Eliza could tell her heart wasn't in it. Ma liked Sundays too.

They turned onto Clark Street and saw the plain one-story building. The church wasn't majestic like the Cathedral, but Eliza wouldn't change it for anything fancier. It was a church for her people with a colored minister, and it felt like home.

Reverend Meachum was greeting his flock at the door. He was a large man with enormous callused hands. His face was broad, making his smiles extra welcoming and his scowls terrifying. He always wore the same simple black suit with a white collar so he wouldn't overawe his flock. The reverend had been a slave before he became a preacher. He'd built barrels and done carpentry so well, that even as a slave he'd earned enough to buy his freedom. Then Reverend Meachum turned around and earned his family's freedom too. Ma often held up his hard work as an example to Eliza.

The First African Baptist Church welcomed every colored person in St. Louis, freedmen and slaves alike, and Reverend Meachum made sure to shake everyone's hand.

"Good morning, Eliza," Reverend Meachum said in his booming voice. "I'm looking forward to your singing today."

"I'll do my best," she promised.

Inside the church was a large room with a door in the back that led to an office and a kitchen. Ma headed purposefully toward the food tables, while Pa took Lizzie with him to talk with some friends. Eliza's destination was the choir. A group of girls ranging from her own age to sixteen was clustered there, chattering away like the blue jays that nested in the trees along the river. She bounded into the circle. But instead of the usual friendly greeting, the girls fell silent. One of the younger girls even took a step back, putting distance between herself and Eliza.

Eliza narrowed her eyes and put her hands on her hips. "What's the matter?" she asked.

Kiki, the unofficial leader of the group and Eliza's chief competition for solos, spoke first. "Is it true?" Kiki's father had been a white slave owner. When he died, he had freed her and her ma. She had light skin and green eyes that Eliza, with her dark complexion and eyes, envied.

"Is what true?" Eliza asked.

Kiki folded her arms and lifted her chin, trying to shame Eliza. "I heard you got the cholera at your place."

Eliza felt as though she'd been slapped. Bad news spread faster than a bloodstain on a white dress. Cholera. And somehow the girls already knew that the Scotts were right in the middle of it.

"My mother told me your ma can't do the potluck table," Kiki said. "And I think maybe you shouldn't sing with us."

"It's Lucy Jones who's sick, not us," Eliza protested. She twisted her neck to see what was happening at the potluck table. Usually Ma was in charge of serving all the food. But today the other women, led by Kiki's mother, were lined up in front of the table, preventing Ma from coming near. Eliza could tell from Ma's hand movements and the set of her chin that she was giving the ladies a piece of her mind.

"You've got nothing to worry about from me or my ma." Eliza snapped her fingers to make sure she had Kiki's attention. "*And* I'll be singing the solo like I always do."

"I remember Lucy," Kiki whispered, her bluster gone. "Is she going to die?"

"She might," Eliza replied. Now that Kiki had backed down, the other girls were looking to Eliza to be the leader again. "Cholera might kill her. Or she might die from the beating she got from the slave catcher Reuben Bartlett." There was a scared murmur from the girls listening. They knew his name. "He thrashed her in front of everybody. She was already caught and ailing, but he did it anyway."

Kiki clapped her hands to her face. "He's here!"

"I just told you that," Eliza said. "If the warden hadn't stopped him, he would have kicked me too."

"No, he's here!" Kiki pointed. Eliza whirled around to see Bartlett standing in the doorway. As the people inside the church saw him, the conversations stopped—the silence spreading like a plague. A dozen or so men stepped forward, putting themselves between Bartlett and the women and children. A baby's cry cracked the silence, only to be hushed by his mother.

Eliza felt her heart beat faster, and she found it hard to

catch her breath. Out of the corner of her eye, she saw a man she didn't know edging along the wall and out the back door. If he was Bartlett's target today, Eliza hoped he would get away.

Reverend Meachum strode down the aisle toward Bartlett. The men parted to let him pass. Reverend Meachum had at least half a foot on Bartlett, and the dark cloth of his suit was strained by his muscles, formed by years of physical labor. He was more than a match for the slave catcher.

Eliza's hands clenched into fists. She wanted to stand up to Bartlett with the reverend. She began to move closer, but a hand on her shoulder stopped her. It was Ma.

"Don't you dare, Eliza!" Ma hissed.

"Mr. Bartlett," Reverend Meachum said, standing toe to toe with the slave hunter.

"Reverend," Bartlett answered. His broad pale face was like a blank book—his expression gave nothing away.

"What are you doing in my church?" Reverend Meachum asked, stepping forward so that Bartlett was forced to move back. "There aren't any fugitives here."

Bartlett's eyes surveyed the crowd. "Maybe, maybe not. There's no harm in looking, is there?"

"You're not welcome." Reverend Meachum moved forward again, and this time half a dozen of his parishioners joined him. They forced Bartlett to retreat, his back pressed against the door. "The wicked have no place in my church, Mr. Bartlett," Reverend Meachum said. His shoulders were squared; Bartlett wasn't the only one prepared for battle.

"'For among my people are found wicked men: they lay wait, as he that setteth snares; they set a trap, they catch men.'"

Ma's voice breathed in Eliza's ear. "Jeremiah 5:26."

"I'll be going now," Bartlett said, as if Reverend Meachum hadn't just called him a wicked man. "But I'll be back whenever I want." He abruptly turned and left.

The door closed behind him, and everyone began talking nervously with bursts of forced laughter. Reverend Meachum's eyes scanned the room until he found Eliza's pa. He beckoned him over. "Dred, get everyone in their seats. The quickest way to wash away the memory of that man is to bathe in God's light."

Pa nodded and began shepherding everyone to a seat. He spoke softly to some of the angrier men and convinced them to sit down. To the elderly, he was soothing and reassuring. Eliza didn't understand how he managed to be so likable and yet still manage to have everyone do what he wanted. Within a few minutes, the congregation was mostly seated.

"Eliza, the reverend will need the choir," Ma said.

"I'm too mad to sing," Eliza said, her voice shaking and her hands still clenched.

Ma gathered Eliza's fists between her hands. "Violence has no place in the Lord's house."

"This is our place, Ma. Bartlett had no right to come here!"

"But he did come here. The sooner you sing, the sooner you'll feel better. And more importantly, you'll help everyone forget him."

Eliza took a deep breath and ordered the girls to their places.

Reverend Meachum moved to the front of the room and greeted the congregation as though Bartlett had never polluted their church. After his opening words, he nodded to the choir to begin their opening hymn: "What Wondrous Love Is This."

As Eliza opened her mouth to sing, she sought out her father in the crowd. Instead of beaming like he usually did, his face was troubled. And Ma was distracted too. By the time they sang the chorus, Eliza found herself calmer—singing always had that power over her. As Eliza sang, the main door in the back of the room opened. Fearing Bartlett had returned, Eliza's voice faltered for a moment. Then she recognized Wilson, the boy from the *Edward Bates*. He saw her looking at him and waved. His bright smile put all the bad things that had happened in the shade. Eliza smiled back.

CHAPTER *Twelve*

AFTER THE SERVICE, ELIZA MADE HER WAY TOWARD WILSON. As
they drew nearer to each other, her tongue tied up in knots.
What was she going to say to him? He waited for her to
speak, but his smile gave her courage.

"You're here," she managed to say.

He glanced around the church, then gave her a cheeky
grin. "I guess I am."

Eliza told herself to stop acting like an idiot. "I mean,
why aren't you on the *Edward Bates*? I thought for sure you
would have sailed by now."

"The hull needs repairs. So I'm on liberty for a couple
of weeks. I remembered you said you liked this church." He
moved in close and lowered his voice. "And I hear folks like
us can get schooling here."

Eliza opened her mouth to tell him about the school, then
she snapped it shut. "I'm not supposed to talk about it."

Wilson looked pleased. "So there *is* a school."

Eliza grimaced. "It's illegal to educate blacks in Missouri."

"I'm a free man," Wilson protested.

"Most of us aren't, not officially." Eliza shrugged. "And Reverend Meachum wouldn't break the law."

"God's law, never!" Reverend Meachum's booming voice behind them made them jump. "The state of Missouri's laws? Sometimes those are meant to be bent."

Eliza grinned. Wilson seemed unsure how to respond, but he took his cue from Eliza and smiled too.

"Who's your friend, Eliza?" Reverend Meachum's words were friendly, but his eyes were watchful.

"This is Wilson," she said. "Wilson, this is Reverend Meachum."

Wilson stuck out his hand. "Wilson Madison. I'm pleased to meet you, sir."

Reverend Meachum gazed at Wilson with cautious approval; he was partial to good manners. "Are you thinking about joining the church?" he asked, shaking Wilson's hand.

"I'd be happy to, but I've mostly come looking for an education. Eliza and I were just talking about your school."

Reverend Meachum lifted his eyebrows. "Is that a fact, Eliza?"

"Wilson, do you mind if I talk to the reverend alone?" she asked hurriedly. After he nodded, Eliza beckoned Reverend Meachum to step away, out of Wilson's earshot. "Wilson already knew about our school," Eliza explained quickly. "I didn't tell him anything."

"Eventually our enemies will realize our school is

hiding in plain sight," Reverend Meachum said. "But with discretion, we can postpone that day as long as possible. Do you vouch for Mr. Wilson?"

Eliza didn't need to think about it. "Sir, he helped me when I needed it," she said.

The corners of Reverend Meachum's lips lifted. "He seems like a fine young man. He can come to the school."

"Thank you, sir!" Eliza said. She beckoned for Wilson to join the conversation. "I'm to bring you to class this afternoon."

Wilson glanced around, his face puzzled. "It's not here?"

"Not anymore," Reverend Meachum said. "We used to have it in the basement, but that didn't sit well with some white folks in town . . ."

"The Committee of One Hundred," Eliza interjected. "They're rich and mean."

"They passed a law to keep slaves from getting an education," Reverend Meachum went on. "Some people would like to expand that law to apply to any colored person. The courts haven't decided that yet. But in the meantime, they closed the school down."

"Then how . . . ?" Wilson asked.

"The reverend is smarter than anybody on the Committee," Eliza bragged. "He figured out a way."

"I'll let Eliza show you," Reverend Meachum said. Lowering his voice, he whispered, "The code word today is 'muskrat.'"

"Yes, sir!" Eliza committed the word to memory.

Reverend Meachum clapped Wilson on the back with his giant hand. Wilson stumbled but kept his balance. "I look forward to talking to you again." The minister moved off to meet with another parishioner.

"'Muskrat'?" Wilson asked.

"You'll see," Eliza promised. "School starts an hour after the service finishes."

Wilson eyes wandered to the potluck table. "I was looking forward to a meal I didn't have to cook."

"Hmmm," Eliza said. "I suppose I could get you some lunch."

"That'd be grand," Wilson beamed.

"Not so fast," Eliza said, holding up a hand. "Did you bring me that cake you promised?"

"I'm afraid not. But I will next time!"

"Wait here." Eliza hurried over to the food table, where Ma was once again in charge. It would take more than a few scared ladies to keep Ma from doing her duty. "I'm going to school, Ma."

"Who's that boy?" Ma asked. Her watchful eyes never missed anything.

"He's a new student. His name is Wilson."

"Where does he come from?" Even Reverend Meachum could take some lessons from Ma about being careful with strangers. "Is he a slave or free?"

"Free, Ma. He works on one of the steamboats. He gave me the drippings last week."

"I want to meet him," Ma said. "I don't want you going

off with a stranger."

"There's no time," Eliza protested. "Besides, Reverend Meachum approved. He said I should bring Wilson to school."

The suspicious expression on Ma's face faded, and she reached under the table for a pail. "That's all right then. Here's your lunch. And I put your pencil and notebook in there too."

"Can Wilson have some too? He's mighty hungry." Eliza's eyes went to Wilson. Her attentions sharpened when she saw that he had been buttonholed by Kiki. Trust Kiki Washington to make a beeline to the new boy!

Ma added more chicken to the pail. "Don't be distracted by this Wilson boy when you should be learning."

Eliza grinned. "I won't!"

"If the reverend likes him, I suppose he could walk you home after school," Ma called after her.

"Bye, Ma." Of course, Eliza would rather die than let Wilson know she lived in a jail. But first things first: it was time to get rid of Kiki.

"It must be interesting to work on a steamboat," Kiki simpered.

"It's all right," Wilson answered. "Ah, here's Eliza." Was Eliza flattering herself, or did she see relief in his face?

"What do you want, Kiki?" Eliza asked, not trying to sweeten the sour in her voice.

"It's Wilson's first day at the school. I'd hate for him not to know anyone," Kiki said, batting her light green eyes at him.

"He knows me," Eliza said.

"Besides you," Kiki went on. "We can go together. What's the code word today?"

"I don't know," Eliza said. Wilson raised his eyebrows. Eliza stared at him, daring Wilson to correct her.

"And you're supposed to be the best student," Kiki scoffed. "Never mind, I'll find out." She bustled away.

"Time to go," Eliza said cheerily. Tugging lightly on Wilson's sleeve, she led him out the main door. She pushed her way through the crowd of parishioners milling about, with Wilson on her heels. On Market Street, she headed toward the water. As the crowd thinned, they were able to walk side by side.

"Isn't the code word 'muskrat'?" he said.

Eliza smacked her hand to her forehead. "Oh my, you're right! Kiki will just have to meet us there."

"And where would 'there' be?" Wilson asked.

"It's a secret," Eliza replied.

The good citizens of St. Louis were dressed in their finest for a Sunday-afternoon walk. It was a sunny day, warm for April, and everyone seemed to be in good spirits. Wilson in his neat vest and trousers and Eliza in her new dress didn't stand out in the crowd at all. As they walked, Wilson peppered her with questions. Eliza just smiled and swung her lunch bucket back and forth. Her pencil and notebook rattled in the bucket. Her secret would keep awhile longer.

They paused outside a popular hotel with columns and wide shallow steps in front. A piano was being played in the lounge. Eliza sang the words under her breath.

"You sing like an angel," Wilson said. "You should be in there singing."

"Girls like me aren't welcome in places like that," Eliza said.

"Maybe, or maybe not. I've heard colored singers on the *Edward Bates*."

Eliza grinned. "Don't you worry. I have my own plans. The world will hear me sing one day."

"How?" he asked.

"I'll tell you," she promised, "when I know you better."

"I'll hold you to that," he said.

Eliza smiled shyly. Someday she might trust Wilson enough to tell him her secrets. In the meantime, it looked like he planned to stick around. Her happy mood was like a shimmering soap bubble.

But that bubble soon popped when a pair of young white men stepped out of the hotel. With a start, Eliza recognized Mark Charless. "Let's go back," she gasped, grabbing Wilson's hand. But it was too late. Mark Charless had seen her.

"If it isn't little Eliza." Turning to his friend, Mark said, "Frank, this is the girl I told you about."

"My aunt's slave?" Frank was taller than Mark and fair instead of dark. His bushy eyebrows hung over pale blue eyes. Where Mark had a weak chin, Frank's jutted out, sharp enough to cut you.

"Your aunt doesn't have any rights over me at all," Eliza insisted.

As if Eliza's words were never spoken, Frank said to Mark, "You're right. She'd fetch a lot of money."

"Enough to stake us for California," Mark agreed, rubbing his thumb and forefinger together.

Eliza's feet twitched as though they knew the smart thing to do was run. "We've got to go," she mumbled.

Frank gestured to Wilson. "Who's he? Does he belong to my aunt too?"

Moving in front of Eliza, Wilson said, "I don't belong to anyone. I'm a free man, and I have the papers to prove it."

If Wilson could be brave, so could Eliza. "And I'm about to be free," she proclaimed. "There's nothing you can do about it."

"No colored talks to me like that." Frank grabbed Eliza's arm and tried to twist it, but she wrenched herself away. Her lunch pail slid off her arm, and the contents spilled out onto the pavement.

"Pencil and paper?" Frank said. "Look, Mark, my slave writes."

"That will hurt her sale price," Mark warned. "Buyers don't like uppity slaves."

Wilson glanced sidelong at Eliza. "I guess they're both hard of hearing. There aren't any slaves here."

"Who taught you to read and write?" Mark asked Eliza.

Eliza clamped her lips together and glared at the young men. Reverend Meachum's first rule was to never draw attention to the school.

"I bet she goes to that school we've heard about," Mark

declared. "The one the Committee can't find."

Eliza knelt down to grab the notebook, but Mark stepped forward and put his shiny black boot square on top of it. "Where's the school?" he demanded.

She pulled the notebook as hard as she could, making Mark stumble back in his heeled boots. "Run!" she shouted to Wilson.

Eliza headed down a side street, her feet pounding against the cobblestones. Wilson was next to her as she darted down one alley, then another. Finally they stopped to catch their breath in an alley near the docks. Eliza looked behind them to make sure they hadn't been followed.

"Why does that man think he owns you?" Wilson asked between gasps.

Eliza dragged air into her sore lungs. She reached out to the wall to steady herself. She was unhappy enough that Wilson had seen the bad blood between her and Mark Charless. But now Mrs. Emerson's nephew knew her face, too. "The blond one is Frank Sanford. His aunt is the one we're suing for our freedom. The other one is Mark Charless. His mother is my ma's boss. They're both hard up for money." She felt light-headed and would have stumbled if Wilson hadn't caught her elbow. She liked how solid he was; "dependable" was the word that best described Wilson, she decided.

"Selling you would solve all their problems?" he asked.

Eliza nodded. "They're wrong. Legally they can't do anything to me."

"No," Wilson said slowly. "But that won't matter if they

send a slave catcher after you. There are plenty who don't care about what's legal. You should tell your parents."

Eliza shook her head hard enough that one of her braids came loose. "They already worry about me all the time."

"They're right to." Wilson's troubled eyes stared into Eliza's. "Those boys looked spoiled and desperate," he warned.

"I'm not scared."

"Then why did you run?" Wilson asked.

Eliza thought fast to come up with a reasonable explanation. "I don't want them making trouble for the school either. So far we've kept the location a secret. We have to go. If we're late, we'll miss it altogether."

At a blessedly slower pace, they left the alley. Ducking between two warehouses, they were at the river. A row of steamboats were docked at the pier, but it was oddly quiet. Instead of the shouts of workers, the hooting of steamboats, and the bustling of wagons, the docks were mostly empty. A dozen cormorants, flying in a V shape, swooped past, trailing the surface of the river with their feet.

Wilson looked about him. "The school is on the docks?" His eyes went to the distant outline of the *Edward Bates*, then back to Eliza's face.

"Nope." She drew Wilson's attention to the sign on the nearest warehouse. It read: CANADIAN FURS. This was the main depot for all the furs coming from the North. "Muskrat is a kind of fur. When the code is 'muskrat,' it means to meet here."

"So the school is in the warehouse?" he guessed.

"Nope." She pointed to the river. Wilson's eyes followed her finger out past the pier to a small steamboat. It was anchored on an island on the Illinois side of the Mississippi, just out of the main lanes for ships traveling on the river. It was a neat ship; its polished wooden sides glistened in the sunlight. At the very end of the pier, four other young people, including Kiki, were watching a rowboat come toward them.

"The *Freedom School*," she announced.

"The school is on a boat?" Wilson asked, delighted.

"The boat is the school. Reverend Meachum is smarter than all one hundred of that committee put together. He figured out that the middle of the river belongs to the U.S. government, not Missouri. The rules about educating us don't apply if we're on the river. But the Committee would still harass us if they knew where it was, so we change the meeting place for the rowboat every week."

Wilson grinned, revealing bright white teeth against his dark skin. "And it's a real school?"

"We've got a teacher *and* a library," Eliza said proudly. "It's my favorite place in the whole world."

Their footsteps made a clumping sound on the wooden pier. The other students turned to see who was arriving. Eliza held up her hand. "It's just me!"

"I bet you knew the password all along!" Kiki accused.

Eliza couldn't quite meet Kiki's eyes. Staring down at the dock, she muttered an apology. Beside her, she heard Wilson snicker. But an indrawn breath made her look up. Kiki's eyes were wary and the other students moved together, like iron filings to a magnet.

A voice behind them made her whirl around. "I know one hundred people or so who would be very interested to know this is where you meet for school." Eliza turned slowly to see Mark Charless and Frank Sanford. Their smug looks made the hairs on the back of Eliza's neck stand on end.

Eliza had led the enemy right to her most prized secret.

CHAPTER *Thirteen*

Kiki glared at Eliza. "How could you bring them here?" she whispered.

"I didn't mean to . . ."

Mark Charless grabbed her arm. "Tell me where the school is."

"I don't know what you're talking about." Even to herself, Eliza's voice sounded tinny and afraid.

"You're a liar," Mark snarled, his gaze scouring the warehouses. "Where is it?"

The splash of a rowboat caught Frank Sanford's attention. His thin lips stretched into a smile. "I bet the school is on the river."

"It's that new steamboat off Bloody Island," Mark said. "No wonder the Committee couldn't find it. We'll soon shut it down now that we know where it is."

"Eliza!" Kiki hissed. "Do something!"

Eliza dug her nails into the palm of her hand—she couldn't lose the school. Worse yet, she couldn't be the one who let the school be lost. She found her courage and said, "In the middle of the river, the United States government makes the rules, not your Committee."

His gaze fixed on the *Freedom School* bobbing at anchor across the water, Mark replied, "The Committee can pass a new law."

The truth of that hit Eliza as hard as a slap; the Committee of One Hundred did what it wanted. She glanced back at the other students. Kiki was glaring at Eliza, but the others—two girls and a boy, all of whom were slaves—looked terrified. Eliza wanted to cry. Now Frank and Mark didn't just have Eliza in their sights—the others were at risk too. She'd put everything in jeopardy.

"We should get the sheriff," Mark said to Frank.

"There's no reason to get the sheriff. We haven't broken any laws," Eliza argued.

"You're all learning to read. That's against the law," Frank said.

"I'm free, so it's perfectly legal." Eliza was startled by Kiki's voice.

Wilson chimed in, "Me too."

Eliza wanted to hug them both, even Kiki. She found her voice again, "In any case, we're not learning in Missouri, and that's all that matters to the law!"

"Maybe you're crossing the river to escape," Frank mused.

He was much sneakier than Mark Charless, who was just mean and stupid. "That's illegal."

"We don't cross the river," Eliza insisted. "We stop in the middle."

The rowboat was coming closer. Abe, Reverend Meachum's right-hand man, expertly pulled at the oars. The muscles in his broad shoulders rippled with the effort of maneuvering the boat across the mighty river. Even from here it was obvious that he was an enormous man.

Frank kept his eyes on Eliza as he said, "Mark, watch them while I get the sheriff."

"You stay. I'll go." Mark had obviously sized up Abe and knew he was outmatched.

A bump against the dock and Abe had arrived. Everyone turned to watch him clamber out of the boat. The wind on the water had whipped his bushy black hair into a crown sticking up from head. Abe's eyes narrowed as he saw the scene on the dock. The other students gathered around him like puppies crowding their mama. Eliza was most relieved of all.

"What's going on here?" Abe asked in his bullfrog voice. He towered over everyone on the dock. His quiet gaze wasn't exactly threatening, but Mark involuntarily took a step backward.

"We're just leaving," Mark squeaked.

"But we've caught them red-handed going to school," Frank protested.

"These children aren't doing anyone any harm. Reverend Meachum's lawyer says we're not breaking any laws," Abe declared. "You leave them alone."

Mark tugged on Frank's sleeve. "We need to go."

Frank gave Mark a contemptuous look, turned, and stalked away. Mark scurried after him.

As soon as they were gone, Abe folded his arms and asked, "How did those men get here?"

"I, um, I . . . ," Eliza stammered, her eyes fixed on Abe's boots.

"Eliza led them right to us!" Kiki accused.

Tears welled in Eliza's eyes. "I didn't mean to."

Wilson put his arm around Eliza. "They didn't follow us. Eliza was careful."

"Not careful enough," Kiki said.

Wilson's arm felt like protection around Eliza's shoulders. Abe sighed. "I suppose it was just a matter of time before they figured it out."

"That's true," Wilson agreed.

Though Eliza felt she didn't deserve Abe's kindness, she was grateful for it.

Abe glanced at the afternoon sun and said, "We'd better go before those troublemakers come back."

Wilson held the rowboat steady for the others to board. Kiki made sure to grab Wilson's arm, but Eliza jumped in unaided, followed by Wilson. He sat next to her in the prow of the boat. With Abe's strong pull on the oars, they were soon in the middle of the river. The cool breeze was refreshing on Eliza's sweaty face, but it couldn't soothe her troubled conscience.

"You love the school, don't you?" Wilson asked.

"Yes," she answered. "But I'm afraid I've ruined everything. I was stupid. Once those men saw my notebook, I should never have come to the docks. The *Freedom School* has to be protected. No one knows that better than I do."

"It's not your fault, Eliza."

Eliza nodded, though she didn't agree. She let her hand trail in the water, not taking it out even when it got icy cold.

The rowboat plowed through the water. Abe kept a sharp eye on the currents. The river seemed slow and safe on the surface, but there were always hazards floating by.

Abe struggled to maneuver the boat close to the steamboat. "Wilson, grab an oar!" he called. Together they fought the tug of the current until they reached the gentler water near the island. "Welcome to Bloody Island."

Wilson's eyes darted to Eliza with a question.

"The island is a no-man's-land," Eliza explained. "It doesn't belong to Missouri or Illinois. Whenever anybody has a duel to fight, they do it there. So they call it Bloody Island. The name has nothing to do with the school."

With a bump, the rowboat pulled alongside the stairs at the side of the *Freedom School*. Wilson jumped out and expertly tied the rowboat to the steamboat. Abe nodded approvingly.

"Oh my, you certainly know your way around boats." The

trill in Kiki's voice set Eliza's teeth on edge. As though Kiki were a queen, she held out her hand to Wilson, and he lifted her out of the boat.

When it was Eliza's turn, Wilson said, "A fellow river rat doesn't need any help."

Eliza saw the jealous expression on Kiki's face and knew she would rather have done laundry every day for a year than ask for assistance.

They climbed the stairs and entered the main room of the steamboat. Eliza's eyes went to every corner, worrying this would be the last time she saw the school.

Wilson touched her arm. "Don't fret. Abe said it would have happened anyway."

Without thinking, she placed her hand over his. "How did you know what was on my mind?" she asked.

Wilson smiled at her. "It's easy to see what you're feeling." He ducked his head to avoid her gaze and looked about the boat.

The inside of the *Freedom School* didn't much resemble a typical steamboat. Instead of staterooms, there was one large room with desks.

Wilson ran his hand appreciatively over the polished desks. "It's beautiful work," he said.

"Reverend Meachum used to be a carpenter, and he made most of this himself." She brought Wilson to the bookcase on one side of the room, filled with two dozen books. "This is our very own library."

"Have you read them all?" he asked.

"Not yet. Someday I will. Miss Stubbs says I'm the best reader."

"She's the teacher?"

Eliza nodded, her finger tracing the title of a book. "She's from Ohio and properly trained."

"It's brave of all of you to break the law just to get an education," Wilson said.

"Is it brave if you are just doing what you want to do more than anything?" Eliza replied.

"School is that important to you?" he asked.

"Can I tell you something I've never told anybody?" she whispered, looking around to make sure Kiki wasn't within earshot.

He laughed. "You know I want to be a pastry chef—I think you owe me a secret."

"Reading is wonderful—but I want an education so I can write songs."

"Writing songs, is that a job?" Wilson asked.

"I met a lady once at church who wrote hymns. Think on it—when you hear a song, you don't know who wrote it. It could be a girl, even a colored girl like me. Imagine people all over America humming my music."

"You are full of surprises," Wilson said. "Why shouldn't you write songs if you want to?"

"Well, I'll need to learn how to write the notes and play a piano—but for now I just sing them in my head."

"Will you sing one of them for me one day?"

Eliza smiled. Nothing would make her more embarrassed. Or happier. "Someday."

———

After the lesson was over, Abe returned the students to the shore. Abe drew Eliza aside. "Don't worry, Eliza," he assured her. "Reverend Meachum will know what to do. We'll probably just lay low for a few weeks, then use a new meeting place."

"Thanks, Abe." Eliza placed her hand on his massive forearm. She slowly turned away; Wilson was waiting for her.

"I'll walk you home," he said.

"That's not necessary," she protested, not wanting him to know where she lived.

"I won't let you go alone," Wilson insisted, holding out his arm. "What if those men are waiting for you?"

Eliza threaded her arm through his as they headed toward the center of town, up Market Street. The long hill was filled with promenading couples, and Eliza pretended she and Wilson were one of them. The more she got to know him, the more she liked him. Someday maybe they would be one of those twosomes. At the corner of Market and Second Streets, she pulled him over to look at Phillips Music Store.

Since it was Sunday, the store was closed. Eliza pressed her face to the glass. She pointed out the instruments and the cases of sheet music in the back of the store.

"Someday your music will be for sale there," Wilson predicted.

Eliza stared at her reflection in the window. She saw a

songwriter. A free girl. A traveler. A reader. She saw the future.

She tore herself from the window, and they continued up Market Street. They talked about the school.

"I can't believe Miss Stubbs gave me a book to read." Wilson patted his satchel where he had stowed the book. "It's called *Robinson Crusoe*."

"You'll like that one," Eliza promised. "Except for maybe the shipwreck."

"Shipwrecks are a fact of life on the water," Wilson said matter-of-factly. "Boilers explode, we can get holed by floating trees and sink—and, of course, there are fires."

Eliza held up a hand. "Stop telling me how dangerous it is! I've always wanted to go somewhere, anywhere, on a steamboat."

He grabbed her hand. "Maybe on the *Edward Bates*?"

Eliza would have liked to say something clever, but they had reached Chestnut Street and the moment she was dreading had arrived. The dome of the courthouse loomed over them. The square was deserted except for a rickety wagon hitched to a horse so thin you could count his ribs. Wilson looked around curiously. "You live around here?" he asked.

"Yes," she answered shortly, as if he wouldn't ask the next question.

"Where?"

She pointed to the building behind the courthouse.

"Isn't that the jail?" Wilson asked, puzzled.

She nodded. "I didn't want to tell you. We're forced to

live there," she explained. She watched his face as she told him the story. When she was done, he was silent for a moment. Would he still like her?

"That's not fair," he said finally. "You and your family should be able to live anywhere you want." He gave her a hard look, almost as scolding as one of Ma's glares. "And you shouldn't be ashamed of something that isn't your fault."

Feeling a weight lift off her shoulders, Eliza agreed. "But in two weeks and one day, we get to go before the judge. Then we won't have to stay here anymore."

The door to the prison swung open. To Eliza's surprise, her father emerged, walking backward. He carried the front end of a stretcher. Mr. Martin followed holding the back. On top of the stretcher was a swaddled bundle, long and narrow. Pa didn't notice Eliza as he and Mr. Martin loaded the stretcher into the waiting wagon.

"Pa?" Eliza asked.

Pa's head whipped around. "Eliza! Get inside. Get inside now." The stricken look on his face told her everything.

"It's Lucy, isn't it?" Eliza asked.

CHAPTER *Fourteen*

Two weeks and a day later.

It was raining again. It had rained every day for a week. But dawn was coming. Eliza could just make out the bars in the cell's narrow window.

Ma still slept. She worked so hard all day, she would fall asleep as soon as her body hit her straw bed. Lizzie was curled in a tiny ball at Eliza's feet, breathing loudly through her mouth. Somehow she had wandered down there in her sleep. Lizzie had a little cold and her nose was stuffed up. Her gentle snuffling was Eliza's lullaby.

Even with that, though, Eliza couldn't sleep. She turned onto one side, then a moment later flipped to the other. It seemed that morning would never come; they had already waited such a long time to be legally freed. A free Eliza Scott could look forward to tomorrow. A colored girl in the jail had no future at all.

Yes, today would be a good day. And the Lord knew they needed some happy news. Since Lucy's death, Pa had convinced Mr. Martin not to accept any more sick prisoners. It had worked—the cholera had stayed out of the jail. That is, until the sheriff had insisted on delivering two men arrested for stealing, even though they were feverish. Soon they were vomiting uncontrollably and their diarrhea wouldn't stop. Mrs. Martin and Pa had worked day and night to save them. They'd tried all the doctor's potions. Ma had painted the window bars with camphor. Pa had coaxed them to drink clean water to replace all the water they were losing to the illness. Eliza didn't understand why boiled water was better than the water from the well, but Pa said all the rain let the town's sewage seep into the well water. That didn't make any sense to Eliza—surely the rain washed the dirt and muck away.

It had broken Pa's heart when both men had died. Mrs. Martin had taken their deaths especially hard. The following morning she had gone to the country to stay with her family. Mrs. Martin wasn't the only one—half the town had run away. The townspeople who were left wore a desperate look and feared their neighbors. Except for the church bells ringing for the dead all day long, the city felt hushed and scared.

The *Freedom School* had not met in weeks, but it had nothing to do with Eliza's mistakes. To keep his people safe from the cholera, Reverend Meachum had closed the church and school until the epidemic was over. The Committee of One Hundred had more important things to do than worry about the school—they met constantly to insist that the city of St. Louis be held accountable for the epidemic. "Stop the deaths," they ordered, as if all their money and power could just cause the cholera to stop. But when Old Man Chouteau, the richest man in town, succumbed, the Committee had to face the fact that the cholera took anyone it pleased—rich, poor, colored, white, or Indian. The cholera was a monster whose appetite was never satisfied.

Eliza knew her family had been lucky not to get sick. But she couldn't help feeling sorry for herself. With no church and no school, she hadn't seen Wilson or any of her choir friends for weeks. Miss Charlotte had told them not to come to her house until the disease ran its course, so Eliza couldn't visit with Sadie either. Pa, Ma, and Lizzie were Eliza's only company.

Eliza's solace was that she had time to work on her rhymes and tunes. Ma and Pa paid them no attention, but Eliza knew her songs were worth writing down. If only she knew how to write music. Or play an instrument other than her voice. Maybe after they were free, Eliza could find a way to learn to play piano.

Eliza wasn't the only one dreaming. The night before, Ma and Pa had been talking about their futures. Eliza had never seen them so happy. Ma wanted her own laundry. Pa could do all the deliveries.

"Setting up a laundry takes money," Eliza pointed out.

"We have savings enough to do it," Pa said.

Eliza's attention sharpened. "If we have money," she asked, "why didn't we just buy our freedom years ago?"

"We tried," Pa said, his voice tired. "But Mrs. Emerson wouldn't take our money. She thinks our family gets more valuable as time passes."

Eliza felt a little sick come up in her throat. "Because the older I get, the better price I'll fetch?"

"Hush," Pa said. "The court won't let that happen."

"So Mrs. Emerson is plain out of luck," Eliza declared.

Eliza wondered about Mrs. Emerson, a woman she could barely remember. Pa said she wasn't a terrible person, just spoiled and apt to use others for her own comfort. Her nephew Frank seemed to be cut from the same cloth. After today, Eliza hoped neither of them would have the power to scare her ever again.

Finally there was enough light at the window to be morning. She slipped out of her blankets and tiptoed out of the cell. Ma had stayed up late the night before ironing their best clothes. She'd left them hanging in the common room. Eliza could fetch them and make one less task for Ma. The sooner they were ready, the sooner they could go to court. Her bare feet padded down the slate floor past the cells of the women trustee prisoners. They were still asleep; they had nothing to look forward to today. Not like the Scotts.

When she returned with the clothes, Ma was already waking Lizzie.

"You're growing so fast," Eliza told her little sister. It was true; the pinafore of her dress barely fit around Lizzie's chest, and the bottom of the skirt brushed her knees. "After today, you can get as tall as you like!"

"As tall as you?" Lizzie asked.

Eliza nodded. Lizzie beamed and stood up straight and proud.

After this morning, it wouldn't matter how tall the Scott girls grew. Once they were legally free, they would be safe from slave catchers and the auction block.

Eliza put on her new dress, her hands trembling so she could hardly fasten the buttons. Ma had found a white petticoat with a small ruffle on the bottom to hold out the bottom of the skirt. Eliza twirled in the hallway, feeling as if she might float away. *Only a free person could feel so light and happy*, she thought. The only flaw in her outfit was her shabby boots, but the ruffle on her skirt hid them, mostly.

Pa looked up and beamed at them when they joined him in the common room. He was shining his boots with a wet rag. Eliza smiled when she saw how dapper he looked in his starched white shirt. Ma had turned the collar and cuffs so cleverly, the shirt looked new.

"Harriet, you look awfully fine in that purple dress," he said.

Eliza added, "You'd never know it was something Miss Charlotte threw away."

Ma touched her fingertips to the lace around her neck. "Stop being foolish—both of you." Ma turned her back and fastened an apron around her waist.

"You can't wear an apron to court, Ma!" Eliza exclaimed.

"I'll take it off before we go. I don't want my dress to get dirty while I make breakfast."

Breakfast was their usual bread with a little meat and vegetable broth to dip it in. But today it was special because it was the last meal they would ever eat as slaves. To celebrate, Ma had a special treat for them, tea sweetened with white sugar. The drink warmed Eliza's whole body. A good sign for today, she decided. In a few hours, they would be free. The only things standing between them and all their dreams were the judge and jury.

The judge. All of a sudden the tea felt like syrup on her tongue—too much of a good thing. Slowly she put the mug back on the table.

Ma's watchful eyes noticed. "Eliza, are you all right?"

"Will the judge want to talk to me?" Eliza asked.

"Of course not," Ma assured her.

Pa reached across the table and put Eliza's mug back in her hand. "Mr. Hall will do all the talking for us. Then the judge will say we're free."

"It's about time," Eliza said, slurping down her tea.

The only one to see them off was Mr. Martin. He clapped Pa on the back and shook his hand. "Dred, we'll miss you here." He nodded to Ma. "Harriet, what will we do without your cooking?"

"Thank you, Mr. Martin," Pa answered in a solemn way. "You've always been decent to us."

Lizzie tugged on Pa's pant leg. "Let's go," she urged him.

"I can't wait another minute."

The adults burst out laughing. But Pa took pity on her, and they set off to the courthouse. It was still drizzling, and Ma and Lizzie broke into a little jog to keep from getting wet. Eliza and Pa walked tall, arm in arm. Under her breath, Eliza hummed her newest tune. Soon she'd be free to write all the music she wanted.

They came into the white marble plaza. At one end was an overlook from which you could see the whole city down to the river. The courthouse filled the other side of the plaza, with its tall columns topped with a dome. Ma and Lizzie waited in the shelter of the entryway.

"The door's locked, Dred," Ma said. "There's no one here." Her voice sounded stretched as tight as wire between two laundry poles. "It's the first day of court. There should be lots of people here."

Something had gone wrong. Eliza felt a cold hard knot in her stomach.

"Don't fret. I'll find out." Pa spied their lawyer looking out over the river. "Mr. Hall!"

The lawyer, in his neat brown suit, approached the court steps. He had no welcoming smile, not even for Lizzie. "I'm sorry, Dred. Judge Hamilton couldn't get enough jurors because of the cholera. Last night he decided to cancel court."

Eliza stared at him, trying to make sense of his words. Their case was scheduled for today. How could the court be closed?

"You should have warned us, Mr. Hall," Ma accused. "How could you let us think . . . we dressed in our best . . . we let the children hope . . ." Ma broke off, tears streaming down her cheeks.

"I'm so very sorry," Mr. Hall said. He turned to Pa, hands outstretched. "I tried to get word to you last night, Dred, but it's impossible to get a message into the jail."

Pa had been standing so proud, but now he slumped, caving in on himself. "It's not the first time we've had to wait," he mumbled. Eliza could hardly bear to see him like that. And Ma? She never cried. A moment ago they had been so happy. So ready to believe the best. To have it snatched away so suddenly was too much.

Eliza finally found her voice. "We shouldn't have to wait!" she cried. "It's not fair. We've already waited too long." She paced about the porch furiously. Stumbling on a loose stone, she picked it up and threw it across the courtyard.

Ma sank down to the pavement, her back against the wall. Pa made as if to go to her, then turned back to Mr. Hall. "What do we do now?" he asked.

Mr. Hall's grim expression warned that the news wasn't good.

"You're going to have to stay at the jail," Mr. Hall said.

"No! We can't go back there!" Eliza shouted.

Lizzie stared at her sister. "Eliza, why are you shouting?"

Pa put his arm around her and murmured, "Stop, Eliza. You're only making it harder for all of us."

Mr. Hall sounded miserable. "It won't be long, Eliza. Only until I can get a court to authorize a bond that will let you out."

"What does that mean?" Pa asked, stroking Eliza's hair.

"The court will hear witnesses that you are good law-abiding folk who won't run away."

"When?" Eliza asked, her voice muffled against Pa's chest.

"The judge has already left town," Mr. Hall answered. "The best we can hope for is a decision in the fall."

Eliza pushed herself away from Pa. "We'll be dead from cholera by fall."

"Eliza, that's enough," Pa said sharply, his words smarting like a whiplash on her skin.

"I'm truly sorry," Mr. Hall repeated, shaking Pa's hand.

As soon as Mr. Hall was out of sight, Pa helped Ma to her feet. She sobbed into his coat while he patted her back.

Eliza walked into the plaza, heedless of the rain. What did it matter if she got wet? What did any of it matter? Nothing they did made any difference. They were going to be slaves forever, locked in the jail until the cholera took them.

A tug on her skirt made her look down. She'd forgotten about Lizzie.

"Eliza, what's wrong?" Lizzie asked. "Why is everyone so sad?"

Eliza scooped Lizzie up in her arms. "We're sad because we're never going to be free," she said, the words bitter on her tongue. "The law is a big lie, and we've been fools to believe in it."

Lizzie's eyes filled with tears.

"Eliza!" Pa took Lizzie from Eliza's arms and held her tight. "Shhh, little one. Eliza didn't mean it. We're going to be free—it's just going to take longer than we thought."

"After today, do you really think the court will ever do the right thing?" Eliza asked bitterly. She couldn't believe she was talking to Pa like this.

His eyes held her gaze for a long moment. "I have to trust in that."

Ma glared at Eliza. "Dred, take Lizzie home," she said.

Pa's eyes went from Eliza's face to Ma's. Without a word, he carried Lizzie away.

"You should be ashamed of yourself," Ma scolded Eliza as soon as Pa was out of earshot. "Upsetting Lizzie like that was cruel."

"I was just telling her the truth. Someone in this family has to face the facts."

"Your father and I have faced more trouble than you will ever know. And if we can be patient, so can you."

Eliza pressed her lips together and didn't answer.

"We're all disappointed. Now let's go home, and you can apologize to Lizzie."

"Home?" Eliza spat the word. Her mother scowled, but Eliza kept talking. "The jail's not home. And I'm never going back."

"You don't have a choice," Ma insisted. "You'll do as I say."

"No," Eliza cried. "I can work for Miss Charlotte and live

in her house instead."

"I already told you no," Ma answered. "You're safer with us."

"I'm not safe at all. None of us are," Eliza shouted. "Lucy's dead. Those two men died too. And Mrs. Martin ran away." As Eliza recited the toll that cholera had taken, she started to hiccup. Her body shuddered and she couldn't breathe. She pushed the final words out. "But we can't run away, can we? We're trapped."

"Calm yourself," Ma said sharply. She took Eliza's arm in a tight grip. "You're getting hysterical. We have to stay in the jail. You can't change that."

"I can change it. I'm not going back. You can't make me." She wrenched her arm away. Ma's fingers left dents in the fleshy part of Eliza's arm. As if her feet were thinking for themselves, Eliza started running.

"Eliza! Get back here right now," her mother shouted.

Eliza kept running. Away from the courthouse and the jail. Away from her family. Away from her life.

CHAPTER *Fifteen*

ELIZA DIDN'T STOP RUNNING UNTIL MA'S FURIOUS CRIES HAD been left behind. She ducked into an empty alley, balanced her hands on her knees and gulped in air. Her dress was spattered with raindrops. The wet she wiped from her eyes was half rain, half tears.

Ma might hate her for it, but Eliza wasn't going to make the same choice as Ma and Pa. She wouldn't just sit and wait for the courts. She was tired of dreaming of a better life and watching it always being snatched away. And most of all, she refused to go back, humiliated and hangdog, to that jail.

Her only option, Eliza decided, was to take Miss Charlotte's job offer, no matter what Ma said. She stood up straight and set off across Market Street. It was odd to be able to walk down the center of the street instead of having to weave through the crowds on the narrow sidewalk. The silence made her feel uneasy; she kept looking over her shoulder. Half the stores were shuttered, even Phillips Music Store.

Miss Charlotte's home wasn't far, and Eliza soon arrived. The large white house's curtains were drawn, as if the house were hiding from the disease that was ravaging the city and making St. Louis a ghost town. Eliza started for the garden gate, then stopped. Why should she go in the side door? She was here at Miss Charlotte's invitation. Taking a deep breath, Eliza deliberately walked up to the front door and lifted the knocker.

For a long time, there was no answer. Eliza glanced around and peered into the window to one side of the door. Maybe the Charlesses had left town? Maybe they were sick? Had she waited too long? Eliza was turning to leave, tears of frustration welling in her eyes, when the door opened a crack.

"Eliza?" Sadie looked exhausted and her white apron showed signs of having been poorly washed. "What are you doing at the front door?" She frowned at Eliza.

"I'm here to see Miss Charlotte." She loved how grown-up she sounded.

"She's still in bed," Sadie said primly.

"Still?"

"You've never worked in a big house." Sadie grimaced. "The mistress gets up when she wants to get up. We never know. Sometimes it's the crack of dawn, sometimes not until noon. But anyway, she's not receiving visitors until the cholera is gone. No one has come to the house for almost a week."

"I'm here about the job Miss Charlotte offered me," Eliza said. "Miss Charlotte wants me to help with the old lady."

Sadie's tired face lightened. "That would be a blessing."

"So tell Miss Charlotte that I can start as soon as she'll have me."

"Your ma's letting you come?" Sadie whispered, leaning in close.

Eliza started to answer with a small shake of her head, then cleared her throat and spoke strongly. "Never mind my ma. I'm making decisions for myself now."

"You never told her about your run-in with Mr. Mark, did you?" Sadie wagged her finger at her. Eliza had never thought Sadie looked much like Cook—but when Sadie took her to task, she could see the resemblance.

Eliza wagged her finger at Sadie. "Just tell Miss Charlotte, Sadie. I'll come back tomorrow."

Eliza hurriedly retreated to the street, all the bravado sinking right out of her body. Her shoulders sagged, and she had to reach for the front gate to stop from folding to the ground. Unwanted tears flowed freely. There was no way Eliza would go back to Ma. No way she was going back to that jail. But where could she go?

After her tears were spent, Eliza scolded herself into action. She couldn't just stand here on the street. She started to walk—away from the Charlesses' house but not toward anywhere in particular. The rain had stopped, and the sun made a pale appearance, as though it weren't sure it would stay.

Her feet took her toward the river. As she started downhill, the muddy sidewalks gave way to the wide wooden planks of the docks. There were more moored ships than Eliza had ever seen at one time. But even with all the ships, there was only a fraction of the usual workers loading and unloading. Eliza's worries about herself faded as she considered whether that was because the workers had sickened or, worse, had died. Mr. Martin had told Pa that six hundred people had died during the past week alone. Six hundred? Where did they put all the bodies? It was a gruesome thought.

A solitary girl was walking toward Eliza, away from the shanties. She was tall, dressed in a plain homespun dress with an apron. Something about her was familiar, but Eliza couldn't pin down the recollection. The girl saw Eliza and headed straight for her.

"Hi, Eliza," she said, a little warily.

Eliza crinkled her forehead. "Celia? Is that you?"

Celia nodded. "You remember me." She was pleased.

"I almost didn't recognize you in a dress," Eliza admitted. "You look pretty."

"Thanks to you." Celia beamed. "I did what you said."

"You went to see Reverend Meachum?" Eliza asked. "I hoped you would."

"When he heard about how we was living, he helped my ma find a job. I'm cleaning the church. And we're moving into a boardinghouse in a few days."

"That's wonderful." Eliza threw her arms around Celia.

Celia stiffened, then hugged her back. "I'm so glad that you're leaving the shantytown."

"Me too." Celia nodded. "It's been even worse since everyone's got sick. I have to go now, but I'm sure I'll see you soon."

"Maybe at the church when it opens again," Eliza promised. With a wave, Celia hurried in the opposite direction. "Hey, Celia!" Eliza called. Celia turned. "Can you sing?"

"Not a bit!" Celia shouted.

"I'll teach you!" Eliza shouted back. She walked on, quite proud of herself for helping Celia find a better life. Surely if she could do that, then getting out of the jail wasn't out of her reach. Still smiling, she climbed the gangplank of the *Edward Bates*, her petticoat brushing against the rope railings.

Wilson was alone, mopping the deck. "Eliza?" He smiled, surprised. "What are you doing here?"

"Um . . . ," she stammered, suddenly realizing how forward it was for her to visit a boy without an invitation, even if she hadn't meant to. Then she burst into tears.

He dropped the mop and raced to her. "What happened?" he asked. "Did you lose the case?"

"No," she managed to eke out while gulping back tears.

"Let's find a quiet place to talk," he said, taking her hand to lead her down the gangplank.

He brought her to a large stone block on the edge of the levee. She told him everything.

"You have to wait until fall?" He sighed. "That's not fair."

Eliza nodded miserably.

Wilson looked out across the river, his eyes fixed on a lone cormorant diving into the river. "Your ma and pa must be very upset."

"Not upset enough. Pa says we've already waited so long, what's a few more months? But I'm tired of waiting."

"Oh, Eliza. I'm sorry."

"Don't be. I'm going to work for my ma's boss. She wants me to look after an old lady. I can live there instead of the jail."

He gripped her arm so hard, she winced. "Didn't you tell me that the man on the docks was the son of your mother's boss?"

Staring at the tops of her scuffed boots, Eliza mumbled, "Yes."

"He lives there too?"

She nodded without speaking.

"Eliza, it's not safe to be near him. You can't go there."

"I'm sure he's left for California by now. No one wants to stay in St. Louis longer than they have to."

Wilson was unconvinced. "What about your family? I've been working for a year, but I miss my own family. Especially with all this sickness." He curled his arm around her shoulder.

"I'll miss them, but I can still see them," Eliza said. "I want to be on my own. Without my ma watching my every move and Lizzie hanging onto my skirts all the time."

"Lizzie's your sister, right?" he asked.

She nodded.

"You don't often meet sisters with the same name."

Eliza leaned back. Her shoulders pressed against his arm. "Ma did it on purpose. If someone asks how old I am, she says Lizzie is still her little baby."

Wilson began to chuckle. "Smart. The younger you seem to be, the safer you are."

"It would please her if I stayed a little girl forever."

"She's protecting you." Wilson's large eyes were thoughtful. "I've seen plenty of slaves transported on the river—not on the *Edward Bates* but on other ships. A lot of them aren't much older than you."

"I'm not a slave," Eliza protested. "We're protected by the law—at least until our case is heard."

"It doesn't matter, if you're unlucky." Wilson hugged her briefly. After a moment, he said, "I've got a new job too."

"What about the *Edward Bates*?" Eliza asked.

"The new job is temporary. Since the *Edward Bates*'s repairs are going to take another few weeks, our captain told us to find some other work. I just got hired by the *Mameluke* for a trip to New Orleans."

"New Orleans!" Eliza said. "Black men aren't safe in Louisiana. My pa says so."

"Black men aren't safe anywhere," Wilson corrected. "But I'll be with the ship. The skipper has a reputation for taking care of his crew."

"How long will you be away?" Eliza had only the foggiest

idea of where New Orleans was.

"We leave tomorrow, and we'll be back ten days after that."

"Ten days!"

"I'll be thinking about you, like I always seem to do these days," Wilson admitted with a shy smile. He pulled a little package out of his pocket. "This is for you."

Her hands were shaky as she took it. No boy had ever given her a gift. "But why?" she asked. "It's not my birthday."

"It was to celebrate your court case," he explained. "But now it's to remind you of me while I'm away." This time it was Wilson who stared down at his boots.

With a wide smile, Eliza unfolded the paper. Inside was a pair of bright green ribbons.

"They're so pretty," she sighed.

"They match your dress," he said. "Let's see." He tied a ribbon around the end of one braid, then the other. His hands were callused on the palms, but the tops of them were soft as they brushed against Eliza's cheek.

"I'll wear them every day you're gone," she promised.

"I'll come see you as soon as we dock," he said.

"The Charlesses might not let me have a visitor," Eliza warned, wondering for the first time what it would be like to work in Miss Charlotte's house. "But there's a gate in the back garden. I could meet you there."

"We need a signal," Wilson said. They agreed on two short whistles followed by a long one.

"Please be careful, Wilson."

"You too. I still wish you were going to any house but that one."

"I'll be fine," Eliza assured him, as if it were a promise she had the power to keep.

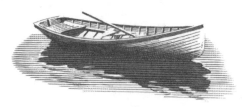

CHAPTER *Sixteen*

"Wake up, Eliza." Ma's voice roused Eliza from a sound sleep.

Opening one eye, Eliza said, "Ma, you made a mistake. It's still dark."

"No mistake. Wake up."

Rubbing her eyes, Eliza saw there was the faintest hint of light from the window. Dawn was close but hadn't arrived yet.

"So we're talking again?" she asked. When Eliza had returned to the jail the night before, Ma had greeted her with dinner and silence that lasted all evening long. Pa had been quiet too, but Eliza could tell he was more disappointed than angry. Eliza had stayed out of their way and played with Lizzie until it was time for bed.

Ma ignored the question. "Get out of bed, young lady. We have a lot to do."

"A lot to do?" Eliza repeated, her mind still in a sleepy fog.

"You're starting at Miss Charlotte's this morning."

Eliza sat bolt upright. "What do you mean?" How much did Ma know?

"Did you think that Miss Charlotte wouldn't ask for my blessing?" Ma said, her pinched face just visible in the dim light. "She sent a note yesterday."

Her whole body perfectly still, Eliza asked, "And?"

"You must want to work for her very much if you would go behind my back." Ma sounded calm, but Eliza heard a tremor in her voice.

"Ma, I just don't want to stay in the jail anymore."

"Your wish is granted, then," Ma said.

Eliza clasped her hands together. "I can go?"

"I'm still against it. You aren't old enough to be on your own."

"I am too."

Ma went on as though Eliza hadn't spoken. "But your pa thinks you'd be healthier in a private house. They have their own water cistern, and Miss Charlotte is keeping strangers away. And we don't dare offend her, especially now that our case is going to take longer than we thought."

Eliza tried to make sense of her change of fortune as she followed Ma into the kitchen. "I took a bath the day before yesterday!" Eliza exclaimed when she saw that Ma had already heated up water on the stove. "You can't expect me to bathe twice in one week."

"Miss Charlotte wants you clean." Ma had Eliza strip right there in the kitchen, saying that no one would be awake for at least an hour. She scrubbed Eliza's skin until it felt raw. When Eliza was clean enough, Ma put a package on the edge of the stove. "And she wants you to wear this."

"Another new dress?"

"More like a uniform," Ma said in a flat voice. Eliza warily opened the package. It was a dress like Sadie wore, blue and made of slave cotton.

"This is a slave's dress," Eliza complained. Her voice got louder. "I'm not a slave."

"Shush," Ma warned. "Of course you aren't a slave."

"Then why should I dress like one?" Eliza demanded. "I'll wear my own dress."

"Miss Charlotte says she knows this is clean."

Eliza put the dress to her nose. Lemon balm. "Ma, I washed this dress myself! I'm wearing a slave's hand-me-down!"

"You got exactly what you asked for," Ma snapped. "Don't complain to me if it's not what you expected."

———

As the sun rose, Ma hurried Eliza through the deserted streets.

"Ma, do we have to walk so fast? No one will even be awake at Miss Charlotte's."

Ma's steps slowed. "Miss Charlotte wants you there first

thing this morning. And her servants will be awake and working, I promise you that."

Eliza remembered how tired Sadie had looked; she'd be glad to have Eliza's help.

"While you're there," Ma warned, "I want you to remember that you aren't a slave—you're being paid."

"What good does that do me?" Eliza said, tripping on the cobblestones slick with morning dew. "The sheriff keeps everything we earn."

"When we're free, we'll get all the money back." Ma's oft-repeated reassurance rang hollow to Eliza's ears.

"If we live that long," Eliza muttered under her breath.

"We certainly will, because we're careful. When you are at Miss Charlotte's, I want you to only drink boiled water. And stay away from anyone who's sick."

"I will, Ma, I swear." They walked half a block before Eliza spoke again. "I didn't even say good-bye to Lizzie."

"It would have upset her."

"Tell her I love her. And tell Pa too."

Ma stopped in the middle of the street. "Eliza Scott, you're only a few blocks away. As soon as the cholera is gone, I'll bring Lizzie to work with me at the house."

"Do you promise?" Ma didn't make promises lightly.

"Yes."

When they arrived at the Charlesses' house, the curtains were drawn, and no one seemed to be stirring.

Ma went down the alley to the locked garden gate. She

knocked loudly. As they waited, she lifted Eliza's chin. "Eliza, please be careful. Be respectful. And don't leave the house." Staring into her daughter's eyes, she said, "You're too young. I never should have agreed."

Eliza threw her arms around her mother and whispered in her ear, "I love you, Ma. I can do this."

Cook opened the door slowly, peering out suspiciously.

"Hello, Harriet," Cook said. "Come in, Eliza." Eliza slipped inside. Ma started to follow, but Cook shook her head heavily. "I'm not allowed to let anyone in."

"But . . ." Ma pressed her lips tightly together.

"You know it's for the best, Harriet."

"Eliza," Ma said. "Be good."

"Ma!"

Before Eliza could say another word, her mother was gone, hurrying down the alley. Cook slammed the gate and shut the bolt. Eliza stared at the gate, tears streaming down her cheeks. "But I didn't even say good-bye."

"It's easier this way. Your ma knows that." Cook handed her a floury rag. "Wipe your face." Her hand, callused from rolling hundreds of pies and biscuits, rested on Eliza's shoulder. "After what happened with Mr. Mark a few weeks ago, I'm surprised she let you come."

Foot raised to take the first step, Eliza stopped. She turned to Cook. "He's not still here, is he?" she asked, barely breathing.

"Of course he is. He lives here." She paused, staring into Eliza's eyes. "Ah, you didn't tell her."

"I thought he'd be in California by now." Eliza glanced behind her at the locked gate. She was trapped.

"No one would give him any money," Cook snorted. "So he's sulking in his room every day. He's trying a new medicine for the cholera—whiskey, and lots of it." She grinned at her own joke, then her smile flattened into a disapproving line. "You've made your own bed, Eliza Scott. And you'd best be avoiding that man."

Eliza matched Cook's snail's pace, humming a tune only she could hear, as if the song would protect her from Mark Charless. Once inside, Cook gave her a gentle shove out the kitchen door. "The mistress is waiting for you in the front parlor."

Eliza smoothed her blue skirt, brushing away some stray flour from Cook's rag. The collar chafed her neck; she wished she could have worn her own clothes. She reached in her pocket and touched Wilson's ribbons. She had hidden them there while Ma's back was turned. She was alone in a strange house, wearing clothes that weren't her own, but she had kept something that belonged only to her. Wilson was alone on a strange ship too. She'd have to be as brave as he was. She tapped on the door.

"Come in." Miss Charlotte sat in the front parlor, near the window overlooking the street. She was crocheting a bright red blanket. Her feet were propped up on a cushioned footstool. An oil lamp was burning on the table next to her, even though the sun was up now. Eliza's eyes couldn't help but drift toward the piano. It still looked unused and lonely.

Eliza's fingers twitched, longing to touch the keys.

"Hello, Eliza." Miss Charlotte's voice made her stand up straight.

Eliza bobbed in a half-curtsy. "Good morning, ma'am."

"You'll be caring for my husband's aunt Sofia," Miss Charlotte said briskly.

"Is she ill?" Eliza asked, concern bringing color to her cheeks. Had she left the jail only to go to a house with cholera?

"No! Of course not." Miss Charlotte waved away that concern. "She's just very old and can be very demanding. Sometimes her mind wanders."

"Wanders?" *How does a mind wander?* Eliza wondered.

"I'm hoping your singing might make her easier to manage."

"I know a lot of songs," Eliza said slowly.

"Excellent. Your job is to keep Aunt Sofia in her room. One less worry for me."

Miss Charlotte's faced seemed drawn and tired. Eliza wasn't surprised. Her husband was always traveling for his business, leaving her alone to care for the house, the family farm, her rotten son, and all the servants.

"You'll take your meals and sleep in Aunt Sofia's room on a pallet," Miss Charlotte explained. "You won't have any reason to leave the room."

"Never?" Eliza asked. Her voice broke on the second syllable. This was just another kind of prison.

"Never." Miss Charlotte's crocheting seemed to require all of her attention. Without looking at Eliza, she said, "My husband's aunt likes to make mischief. But it's not as if she's ever hurt anyone."

Eliza's eyes went wide as Miss Charlotte rang a little silver bell. Sadie appeared in a few seconds. "Sadie, take Eliza to Miss Sofia's room."

"But . . . ," Eliza protested.

Miss Charlotte waved her away.

Walking upstairs to Miss Sofia's room, Eliza squeezed Sadie's hand. "How bad is this Miss Sofia?" She paused. "Is she dangerous?"

"She's not that bad," Sadie said, not meeting Eliza's eyes. She broke away and hurried upstairs. Miss Sofia's room was at the top of the stairs facing the garden. Sadie pulled a large key from her pocket, unlocked the door, then gave it to Eliza.

Eliza felt the heft of the key in her palm. "Why do I need this?" Eliza asked, clutching the heavy key in her palm.

"Miss Charlotte's orders," Sadie answered. "Miss Sofia isn't allowed out by herself. It's your job to keep her inside."

"She's a prisoner?" Eliza asked. Her head was spinning. This morning she had woken up in a cell, but now she was the jailer. She wished she had a moment to stop and think, but Sadie was turning the doorknob.

She gave Eliza a shove through the open door. "Miss Charlotte's orders," she said. "And lock the door behind you."

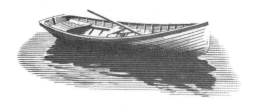

CHAPTER *Seventeen*

THE CURTAINS WERE DRAWN AND THE ROOM WAS TOO DIM TO make out anything or anyone. Eliza stumbled inside, stretching her hands in front of her. The smell of old woman, past meals, and a neglected chamber pot hit Eliza like a smack on the nose.

"Who's there?" The quavering voice came from the opposite side of the room.

"Miss Sofia," Sadie called from the hall. "This here's Eliza."

"Get out!" Miss Sofia screeched. "I want to be alone!"

"Sadie, don't leave me!"

"Good luck, Eliza!" Sadie pulled the door shut. "Don't forget to lock the door."

Sadie's footsteps on the stairs faded away. Eliza was alone. She put the key in the door but didn't lock it. *Like home,* she thought. *Another unlocked cell.* Her eyes scanned the darkened room. Where was Miss Sofia hiding? What if she snuck up behind Eliza and struck her? Eliza whirled around, but she couldn't see a thing.

"Are you still there?" the woman called out. "I have a pistol and I know how to use it."

"Don't shoot me!" Eliza cried. She backed up until her spine was pressed against the door. Her body was rigid, braced against a bullet. No one had said anything about a gun!

"Why shouldn't I?" the voice demanded. "You want to lock me away like the rest of them."

"I'm not like that," Eliza insisted. "I hate being locked up."

"I heard the key in the door," the voice accused.

"I was told to do that," Eliza answered, "but I didn't lock it."

"You disobeyed Charlotte's orders?" There was a new note in the woman's voice—curiosity.

"Yes, ma'am," Eliza said with a gulp. "But I'm going to lock the door if I decide you're crazy."

A short burst of surprised laughter echoed in the dark room. Eliza's body relaxed a little.

"Do you really have a pistol?" Eliza asked.

"Yes, so you'd best answer my questions," the voice ordered.

"Why don't we let in some light," Eliza suggested. The old woman didn't protest. Eliza moved past the bed, stubbing her toe on a rocking chair and bumping into a table. To ease the sharp pain, she hummed as she crossed to the window and pulled the curtains aside. The window faced east, and the morning sun struck the darkness away.

When she turned to take in her new home, Eliza saw a huge bed that took up half the room. Miss Sofia looked like a doll, sitting upright in that enormous bed. Her back hardly touched the pillows. She was the oldest woman Eliza had ever seen. The wrinkles on her face looked like a fine white porcelain cup had been shattered and then glued together. Her robe was held closed by one hand at the neck and the other hand stroked a pistol.

Miss Sofia blinked against the light, peering at Eliza. "You're a Negro!" she exclaimed.

Eliza narrowed her eyes. "So?"

"I've told Charlotte I don't want any of her slaves."

"Why not?" Eliza couldn't keep the edge out of her voice.

"Slavery is an abomination," Miss Sofia pronounced.

Eliza felt the knot in her stomach dissolve like a piece of hard candy on the tongue. "You're an abolitionist?"

"All the Charlesses are!" Miss Sofia went on. "So leave now, and tell Charlotte I will not have you or any other slave." A glint appeared in the old woman's eyes, and she fingered the gun.

Eliza placed her hands on her hips and grinned. "I'm not a slave, I was born free. Miss Charlotte *hired* me to look after you."

"Hired you, did she?"

"Yes, ma'am."

Miss Sofia smiled slowly, slid the pistol under her pillow,

and patted the bed. "Where did my niece find you, Eliza?" Miss Sofia asked.

"My pa used to be one of Miss Charlotte's slaves."

"You're Dred Scott's daughter!" Miss Sofia jabbed a finger toward Eliza as if she had placed Eliza on a map in her mind. "I didn't realize you were quite this old."

"My ma would be pleased to hear that," Eliza said.

Miss Sofia's eyes stayed on Eliza's face. "I'm sure she would. So you're a freedom litigant. Where do you live?"

Eliza closed her eyes as she answered, "In the jail."

"The jail?" Miss Sofia's voice was like spitting nails. "How despicable to punish people for trying to get what's owed them under the law."

Eliza couldn't speak past the sudden lump in her throat. Sometimes she forgot how much her parents had risked; she wished she'd been more grateful.

"Sit down. I want to hear about the case. Is Charlotte still paying for your lawyer?"

"I think so." Eliza perched on the edge of the feather mattress. Her body sank at least six inches—she'd never felt anything so soft. She could imagine the fun she and Lizzie would have jumping on it. She couldn't think of Lizzie now; she'd only start to cry. "But I've never understood why."

"Poor Charlotte feels guilty, of course. She knows slavery is terrible, but she can't live without the comfortable life the slaves make for her. She's misguided, but for all that she's a decent woman." Miss Sofia fixed a beady eye on Eliza. "Don't repeat that!"

Eliza nodded solemnly. She was beginning to like Miss Sofia.

"She does treat her slaves well," Eliza offered, although it went against her grain to defend a slave owner, even one as kind as Miss Charlotte.

Miss Sofia snorted. "If she cares about her slaves, she should free them. The family can afford it."

"I'm grateful she's helping us," Eliza admitted. "But why is it a secret?"

"She doesn't want her fancy friends to know," Miss Sofia confided. "Your owner, Mrs. Emerson, was born a Sanford, one of the most powerful families in the city."

"I've met Frank Sanford." Eliza's voice came out in a squeak.

"The black sheep of the family—even though he's barely twenty. I hear he wants to go west with my idiot grandnephew, Mark, if only they had the money."

"You know a lot for someone who doesn't leave her room."

"I hear a lot." Miss Sofia lifted her eyebrows, inviting Eliza to be in on the secret. "Especially if voices are raised."

"Miss Charlotte and Mark." Eliza wasn't guessing.

"You've heard them too?"

"When I do the laundry in the garden."

Miss Sofia jabbed at Eliza with a claw-like finger. "That was you, singing!"

Her eyes fixed on Miss Sofia's gnarled hand, Eliza answered, "Yes, that was me."

"I take back what I said about Charlotte. She did right

by me when she found you." Suddenly, Miss Sofia fell back against the pillows. "Sing me a song."

Eliza thought for a moment and began to sing one of her favorites. Best of all, she had heard that it was written by a woman.

> *Wild roved an Indian girl,*
> *Bright Alfarata,*
> *Where sweep the waters*
> *Of the blue Juniata!*
> *Swift as an antelope*
> *Through the forest going,*
> *Loose were her jetty locks,*
> *In many tresses flowing.*
>
> *Gay was the mountain song*
> *Of bright Alfarata,*
> *Where sweep the waters*
> *Of the blue Juniata.*
> *"Strong and true my arrows are,*
> *In my painted quiver,*
> *Swift goes my light canoe*
> *Adown the rapid river."*

"I like that song," Miss Sofia said with a satisfied sigh. She was snoring softly before Eliza finished the final stanza.

Eliza pushed herself off the bed and looked around the room. She'd already noticed its plainness and wondered if that was Miss Sofia's choice or Miss Charlotte's. There was a carpet on the floor, with a pattern of big roses like the one in the parlor, but this carpet had faded in the bright sun and had bald patches. Eliza sniffed. The smell wasn't so overpowering now that her nose had gotten used to it, but the room still felt musty. Eliza threw open the window and breathed deeply.

The room looked out on the garden, with a view of the alley behind it. It was drizzling, and the cool breeze carried a dampness that revived her. Miss Sofia stirred in her bed but didn't wake. Eliza noticed a layer of dust on the table and lint and grime in every corner. Well, if Ma had taught her anything, it was how to clean.

She searched the room for a broom, but there wasn't one. She considered the door. Mark Charless might be on the other side—she was safer in here. But she wanted to do a good job to repay Miss Charlotte for her kindness. An idea popped into Eliza's head. Dare she do it? Gingerly, she slipped her hand under Miss Sofia's pillow. She slid the gun out. Taking it to the window, she opened the barrel. Pa had learned about guns on the frontier, and he'd shown her how they worked.

She started to laugh. The gun wasn't loaded. *Good for Miss Sofia*, she thought. She'd used the gun to scare Eliza half to death; Eliza would do the same to Mark if he made any trouble. She stuck the gun in her pocket and opened the door a crack.

Sadie was on the stairs, polishing the banister. "I've been wondering about you," she confessed. "What happened with Miss Sofia?"

"What did you think would happen when you pushed me into a room with a crazy lady holding a gun?" Eliza snapped.

Sadie's mouth dropped open. "A gun? Eliza, I swear I didn't know she had a gun. Are you all right?"

"I am," Eliza assured her. "Actually, the old lady's not that bad. But her room is filthy. Where can I find a broom?"

"It's not our fault it's dirty." Sadie straightened up and glared at Eliza. "Every time we go in there, she chases us out!"

"Well, it's my job now," Eliza said impatiently. "The broom?"

After Eliza collected an armful of cleaning tools, she headed back to the room. Just as she reached Miss Sofia's door, Mark stumbled down the steps, his breath reeking of whiskey. He blinked at Eliza with bloodshot eyes, shaking his head as though he were trying to clear his mind.

"You! What are you doing here?" Mark mumbled, rubbing his eyes as if he didn't believe what he was seeing.

"Your mother hired me," Eliza replied, her voice quaking.

He moved between her and the door. "You're the reason I'm trapped here," he accused, slurring his words. "If it weren't for you, I'd be in California by now." Faster than she would have thought possible, he struck at her face. Eliza dodged his fist and it slammed into the wall. He cried out in pain.

"I'll kill you for that," he snarled, spitting as he spoke. He started for her.

Dropping the cleaning supplies to the floor, Eliza reached for the gun.

CHAPTER *Eighteen*

S HE PULLED THE GUN OUT OF HER POCKET AND POINTED IT AT his chest. Mark's eyes locked on the barrel. They could both see her hand was trembling.

"Let me pass," Eliza demanded.

"You wouldn't dare," he challenged her.

"Are you sure?" she asked. Even though she was only a young colored girl who wasn't quite free and he was a twenty-year-old white son of a big house, she felt that he might back down. His wits were addled by alcohol, and she knew from that day on the docks he wasn't very brave.

Glaring at her, he stepped away, hands raised in the air.

Her eyes fixed on him, she hugged the wall with her spine. She slid past him to Miss Sofia's room. Thank goodness she had left it unlocked. She slipped inside, slammed the door, and turned the key. Eliza was shaking so hard she could barely stand. The gun dropped from her hand to the floor. *Ma is going to kill me*, she thought. *Keep your head down. Be respectful. Stay safe.* Eliza had broken every rule on her first day.

Miss Sofia sat up. "Eliza?" she called. She saw Eliza by the door. "What's going on?"

"Aunt Sofia!" Mark pounded loudly on the door. "Let me in. She has a gun. She's dangerous!"

"Eliza, what's wrong with Mark?" Miss Sofia's eyes lit on the gun at Eliza's feet. She felt under her pillow, then angrily asked, "Is that my gun?"

Eliza ran to the bed and grabbed Miss Sofia's hand. "I can explain, but please don't let him in. He'll hurt me."

"Open this door!" Mark shouted.

"Go away, Mark," Miss Sofia screeched. "Or I'll have your father cut your allowance. Again!"

Mark stopped hammering at the door. Eliza heard him trip and stumble. Then it was silent.

Eliza slumped over Miss Sofia's pillow, letting the cool linen draw the heat from her face.

Miss Sofia patted her back. "Aren't you full of surprises? You've been here a few hours, and you're already drawing a gun on my grandnephew?" To Eliza's relief, the old woman sounded more bemused than angry.

"We've met before," Eliza admitted. She pushed herself away from the bed, forcing herself to inhale and exhale slowly until she was breathing normally.

"To meet him is to want to shoot him," Miss Sofia agreed. "You're going to tell me the whole story, but first give me the gun. Not that it would have done you much good . . ."

"I knew it wasn't loaded," Eliza hurried to say. "I just

wanted to get some cleaning supplies. I was afraid I'd run into Mr. Mark, so I borrowed it to scare him off." She fetched the gun, and Miss Sofia slid it under her pillow.

"Don't leave anything out," Miss Sofia ordered. "You can't keep secrets from me—not if you want me to protect you."

For all of Miss Sofia's enjoyment of the situation, Eliza could tell she was worried. A colored girl just didn't point a gun at a white gentleman without consequences. She began to tell her story. And Miss Sofia was a gratifying listener, hanging on every word, prompting Eliza to go on whenever she hesitated. It was an unexpected relief to confide in someone else. When Eliza was finished, Miss Sofia leaned back against her pillows and looked toward the ceiling.

"You seem to find trouble wherever you go," Miss Sofia noted. "So far, you've run afoul of Mark, Frank Sanford, the Committee of One Hundred, and a slave catcher. Not to mention the cholera."

"I know," Eliza whispered. "Ma's going to kill me." She paused, silently thinking Wilson would too. "What do I do now? Mark won't forget what I did."

"His worst vice is alcohol," Miss Sofia replied. "That's your salvation. He's probably too drunk to remember."

"I hope so," Eliza said. She didn't say it aloud, but it seemed to her that Mark blamed Eliza for his problems. He wasn't going to forget about her presence in his own house.

One day followed another at the Charlesses' house. Eliza kept track by counting down the days until Wilson's ship might come back. Eliza's duties were easy, and she and Miss Sofia soon became fast friends. Miss Sofia taught Eliza card games, and they played poker and all fours for hours. Ma would have a fit if she knew Eliza was playing cards, but Eliza rather liked pitting her wits against the old lady's.

Miss Sofia's eyesight wasn't good, so she would sit near the window in the morning when the light was strongest, holding her embroidery hoop close to her face. Eliza would sort through the skeins of threads, holding the various colors to her skin, imagining wearing a bright yellow or a dark red—something that would look pretty with her hair ribbons. *Maybe someday,* she thought. But for now, time was standing still. Every day felt like the one before, although every day that passed meant Wilson was closer to coming back to St. Louis.

Eliza missed her family, but every few days she received a note from the jail, dictated by Ma and penned by Mr. Martin. Ma's notes were so short that Eliza worried she was still angry. Eliza would report back that Miss Charlotte's house was free of the disease and the job was going well.

Most afternoons Eliza would tell Miss Sofia stories. About doing laundry on the riverbank or going to the *Freedom School.* In her turn, Eliza heard the story of Miss Charlotte's wedding and how she and Mr. Charless had married against the wishes of both families.

"All the Charlesses are abolitionists, and we don't marry slave owners," Miss Sofia said. "But Charlotte and Joseph were fond of each other." Her voice soured as though treating Miss Charlotte fairly upset her stomach. "She's made him a good wife. Except for spoiling that no-good Mark."

"I wish she would spoil him a little more and give him money to go away," Eliza said. As the words left her mouth, she realized that Miss Sofia no longer felt like her charge, but more like a friend.

Miss Sofia placed her hand over Eliza's. "I know you wish him gone. Has he bothered you again?"

"I've been careful," Eliza answered.

"That's a smart girl."

One early morning before Miss Sofia woke up, Eliza was humming and scribbling down her song at the table. She thought the lyrics were coming along, but she was having trouble with the tune.

> *I was born on the river in the pouring rain,*
> *And wandering is my middle name.*
> *As long as I live, my strength I will give*
> *To the river that's never the same.*

"*Dum, dum, dumedy dum,*" she hummed. She shook her head in frustration. That wasn't right. The cadence was wrong.

"Child, what are you singing?" Miss Sofia's sleepy voice was curious.

Eliza crumpled the paper into a little ball. "It's just something I made up," she admitted.

"You write songs?" Miss Sofia sat up in bed; Eliza hurried to her side to help.

"I'd like to. Someday," Eliza explained, as she fluffed the pillows behind Miss Sofia's back. "But first I need to learn to read and write musical notes so I can get the tune out of my head and onto paper."

"I can teach you," Miss Sofia said. "My piano is downstairs."

"I've seen it," Eliza replied, trying to hide her longing. "But it wouldn't be right for me to play it." Ma would have some sharp words for Eliza if she found out. A colored girl didn't play her employer's piano.

"Nonsense," Miss Sofia insisted, throwing back her blanket. "Besides, no one is up this early."

"But it will wake the house."

Miss Sofia shook her head, then led the way downstairs like a soldier commanding a raiding party. She was more spry on her feet than Eliza would have expected.

They snuck into the parlor, and Miss Sofia had Eliza sit at the piano. The instrument was polished and perfect, like a dream just within reach. Eliza was afraid if she closed her eyes, the piano would disappear in a puff of smoke. She ran her fingers over the smooth keys.

"Get those pillows," Miss Sofia said, pointing to the parlor chairs. "Now help me lift the top of the piano." Eliza watched, confused, as Miss Sofia put the pillows on top of the wooden levers inside the piano.

"Listen!" Miss Sofia said with a mischievous smile. She pressed down on a key. The noise came out of the piano as a muffled *plunk*. "Now no one needs to know what we're doing."

Early morning soon became Eliza's favorite time of day. They would slip downstairs, and Miss Sofia would unlock the piano's secrets for her. When Miss Sofia slept, Eliza would pretend the table was a keyboard and practice her notes. Every time she learned a new note or chord, Eliza knew she was building toward her future. She wished she could play her songs for Ma, but then again, Ma would think Eliza was taking liberties by learning the piano at all.

One evening Miss Sofia and Eliza sat by the window in her room as dusk was falling. Soon they would have to shut the windows against the insects of summer—but for now they were enjoying that moment just after a rainstorm when the world is perfectly quiet except for the dripping of water off the roof.

A whistling floated up through the outside sounds to Eliza and Miss Sofia. Two short bursts, then a long one.

"Wilson's back!"

"Your beau?" Miss Sofia asked. Eliza had told her all about Wilson Madison.

"He's not my beau; he's my friend," Eliza replied, her cheeks hot. The whistling sounded again. "But he kept his promise." She hesitated. "Would you mind . . . ?"

"Don't keep him waiting. Go!" Miss Sofia said, giving Eliza a little shove.

Eliza opened the door a crack and peered outside.

The hall was empty. She hurried through the kitchen so quickly that Cook didn't even look up from her chopping. She was making chicken soup for the neighbors next door. Miss Charlotte had heard they were ailing. She forbade the household to have any contact with them, but she also gave instructions for Cook's soup to be left on their doorstep. It was the most the Charlesses would do for their neighbors. Eliza didn't consider it a lot. Her own parents, who had so little, never hesitated to help, even a stranger. Ma and Pa knew the risks better than anyone, but they did it anyway. It was a miracle they hadn't gotten sick. Eliza's breath caught—what if they were sick? Maybe Wilson was bringing bad news?

Fear gave her feet even more speed. She hurried down the steps to the garden. She wasn't allowed to open the gate, but she could see Wilson through the wood slats. "Wilson?"

"Eliza! How are you?"

"I'm good," she said impatiently. "Are you all right? Is my family sick?"

He quickly reassured her. "Everyone is well. I saw your pa this morning."

She exhaled with relief.

"Are you safe here?" he asked. "Has Mark given you any trouble?" She winced at the worry she heard in his words.

"No, he's been fine," she lied. "I like the job. How is the *Mameluke*?"

"It's not bad. I prefer the *Edward Bates* though. Aren't you going to let me in?"

"I can't. It's against the rules," Eliza said. "At least I get to see you. Are you back for good?"

"No. We're transporting slaves to New Orleans day after tomorrow."

Eliza pressed her forehead against the wooden gate. "I wish you didn't have to go."

"Eliza!" It was Cook. "What are you doing out of Miss Sofia's room?"

"Miss Sofia gave me permission!" Eliza replied.

"Then you might as well bring up her tray."

Eliza turned back to Wilson, but a commotion starting in the alley stopped her in her tracks. "Wilson," she asked. "What's happening?"

He looked behind him, and for a moment he went still. "Wait here."

"Wilson!" She stood on her toes, trying to see over the fence. She said his name again, but he didn't answer.

When Wilson came back, she could tell from his face that the news wasn't good.

He reached out and put his hand on hers. "I'm sorry," he said. "But your neighbors are dead. That was the wagon collecting the bodies."

"I have to tell Miss Charlotte." She squeezed Wilson's hand, then ran into the house.

"Be safe, Eliza!" he called after her.

"You too!" she cried over her shoulder. Eliza raced through the kitchen to the parlor. The door was shut and she didn't dare burst in. Eliza rapped on the door, her knuckles smarting against the wood.

"Come in." Miss Charlotte sat in her usual chair by the window, a lamp lighting her work. She put down her knitting when she saw Eliza's face. "Eliza, is something wrong with Aunt Sofia?"

"The neighbors across the alley . . ." The words tumbled from her mouth. "Cholera's killed them all!"

"The Fitzpatricks are dead?" Miss Charlotte's face went ghostly pale. "But they were so careful."

"Mother, now will you leave the city?" Mark's voice, half slurred with drink, was chilling. Eliza peered into the shadows at the edge of the room; she could just make out his body lying on a sofa. "Or do we need to start dying too?" he asked.

Miss Charlotte pressed her palms on the arms of her plush chair and pushed herself up. "Yes. It's time to leave St. Louis and go to the farm. I've delayed too long already. I had hoped we'd be able to ride out the disease."

"I can have the carriage brought 'round, and we'll leave in an hour," Mark said.

"We have to bring clothes and bedding and dry goods. Today is too soon, but perhaps tomorrow," Miss Charlotte said.

"Tomorrow may be too late," Mark warned. "We need to go now. The others can follow."

"I'm responsible for my slaves. I won't leave them for the

cholera to take." Miss Charlotte turned to Eliza. "Tell Aunt Sofia that we'll be going to the farm tomorrow."

Eliza hadn't even known that Miss Charlotte was considering moving to the farm, which she knew was miles away. Ma had always warned her not to leave the city. She stood stock-still trying to think of what to say.

"What are you waiting for?" Mark asked.

Taking hold of herself, Eliza said, "Miss Charlotte, I'm sorry, but I have to stay here. Ma won't let me leave the city."

"That won't do. I need you to mind Aunt Sofia."

Eliza had an idea that would protect everyone. "Then can my parents and Lizzie come with us?"

Mark burst out into mean laughter.

Miss Charlotte was kinder, but she shook her head. "I'm sorry, Eliza. But we can only bring our own people."

"But . . ." Eliza asked herself what Ma would say, and for once she didn't have an answer. Ma would want Eliza to keep safe and be obedient to Miss Charlotte. So Eliza should go. On the other hand, to leave would break two of Ma's most important rules: Stay close to the family and stay in the city. "Can I think about it?" she asked.

"Eliza, your mother trusted me to take care of you," Miss Charlotte said sternly. "You're coming with us."

Blinking back tears, Eliza hesitated.

"Just go, you stupid girl!" Mark shouted.

Eliza looked to his mother for help, but Miss Charlotte said nothing.

The heat rushed to Eliza's face, and she backed out of the room. Out in the hall, she stopped. Her breath came quickly, and she felt dizzy. Eliza desperately needed her mother to tell her what to do.

CHAPTER *Nineteen*

By NOON THE NEXT MORNING, THE HOUSEHOLD GOODS WERE packed into a wagon and ready to travel. Although the journey was less than ten miles, Cook had prepared a picnic basket for the family, and Eliza carefully placed it inside the fancy carriage. Miss Charlotte, Miss Sofia, and Mr. Mark climbed into the carriage, settling themselves into the cushioned seats, while Eliza joined Miss Charlotte's slaves behind the wagon.

"The old lady has taken to you so strong that I thought she might ask for you," Sadie said.

"She did," Eliza confided with a crooked grin. "But Mark said no."

"He's so mean," Sadie said loyally.

"I'd rather walk than be stuck in a carriage with him."

The carriage and wagon started to lumber down the deserted street, heading out of the city. Half a dozen slaves and Eliza followed. They were leaving the house empty except for Jasper, one of Miss Charlotte's oldest slaves. Eliza thought he was too feeble to guard the house, but it wasn't her place to offer an opinion.

Eliza wanted to enjoy the fine weather—it was the first time she had been outside the garden since she came to the Charless house—but all she could think of was her family.

Ma and Pa would be frantic when they discovered she was gone. And Eliza would worry every day until she heard from them. Miss Charlotte had said she couldn't spare anyone to send a message to Eliza's parents. Miss Sofia had been sympathetic, but even she had been too preoccupied with her own packing to help. For the first time, Eliza understood what Ma had tried to tell her. Miss Charlotte and Miss Sofia were kind, but their needs would always be more important than Eliza's.

She caught a glimpse of the courthouse dome, knowing the jail lived in its shadow. It was so close. Without thinking, she took a few steps in that direction. Sadie pulled her back.

"Miss Charlotte will be angry if you disobey her," she warned.

The procession had traveled only a few blocks from the house when the carriage stopped. The door swung open and Mark Charless jumped out.

"What is he doing?" Eliza asked Sadie.

"He probably forgot his bottle of whiskey," Sadie giggled.

Eliza smiled in return, but her eyes were fixed on Mark. He was arguing with the ladies in the carriage. After a few moments, the carriage lurched forward, leaving Mark behind. He waited until the slaves caught up to him and then beckoned to Eliza. Reluctantly she let the others move on without her, leaving her alone with Mark.

"Oh, Eliza," he said a little too casually, "Aunt Sofia forgot her crocheting hooks."

"I packed them in her trunk."

"She's sure they're still at the house," Mark insisted. The smell of whiskey wafted off his breath, and she almost gagged. "If you're quick to fetch them, you can catch up with us easily."

Her mind worked furiously. What was he up to? He might have invented this errand just to make her life difficult. But what if it was true and Miss Sofia wanted Eliza to return to the house? "I'll ask Sadie to go with me."

"There's no use in two of you going."

"But . . ."

"Just do as I say." Mark's voice was loud.

"Yes, sir." The carriage and the group were farther away now. Sadie glanced back. Eliza waved, then turned to run. Before she had gone too far, Eliza looked over her shoulder. She caught her breath when she saw Mark still standing in the middle of the road, watching her. Luckily when she turned the corner, he was out of sight.

She soon reached the house and let herself in by the garden gate. Jasper was sitting in the garden whittling a stick.

"Back so soon?" he asked.

"Miss Sofia forgot something," she called.

In Miss Sofia's room, Eliza frantically searched for

the cloth case with the full set of embroidery tools. It was nowhere to be found. This was taking too long. She had to hurry and rejoin the others before they got too far away. Just in case, she tucked a spare crochet hook in her skirt pocket. Then she ran headlong down the stairs, banging the kitchen door behind her. Jasper was gone, but she didn't have time to wonder about him or to say good-bye. She pulled on the gate. To her surprise, it didn't budge. She tugged harder.

Rattling the gate, she called, "Jasper! The gate is stuck. Come . . ."

Suddenly Eliza was pushed face-first into the gate. Her head rang from the blow. A white man's hands grabbed and dragged her back into the garden.

"Let me go!" she cried. No matter how she struggled, he held tight. She bent her neck and bit his arm as hard as she could. He howled with pain and his grip loosened. Eliza wrenched herself away.

"Help! Help!" she screamed as she whirled around to face her attacker. Wearing the clothes of a dockworker, he was a stranger. He lunged for her and she tried to run. Stumbling, she almost fell. She gasped when she saw she had tripped over Jasper, who lay unconscious on the grass. The house was empty, Jasper was hurt, and the neighbors were dead. Who could possibly help her now?

"Who are you?" Eliza demanded, failing to keep the fear out of her voice. "What do you want?"

Looking past her, the man shouted, "Jimmy, grab her!"

There was another one? Eliza turned to face the second man, but he had already pinned her arms behind her back. She jabbed her elbow backward into his stomach; he was a big man and that was as high as her elbow could reach. He grunted, but his grip didn't loosen for an instant. She kicked back but her captor only held her tighter.

"She bit me!" the first man whined, examining his bloody arm.

"Oh, poor Amos, did the little colored girl hurt you?" Jimmy asked. His breath was foul and warm next to Eliza's cheek. She twisted and kicked, but his hands held her like a vise.

"Just watch her. She's sneaky." The man called Amos held a gray sack in his hand.

"She'll soon learn better where's she's going," Jimmy smirked.

"What do you want with me?" Eliza panted.

Without any warning, Amos slapped her hard with the back of his hand. "Shut your mouth," he demanded, then slipped the sack over her head. Eliza couldn't see anything. The smell of mildew and rot filled her nose. She clawed at her throat as a drawstring pulled snug around her neck. Her screams were muffled by the cloth.

A loop of rope was dropped over her wrists. She gasped as the rope was jerked tight, cutting into her skin. Hands bound in front of her, Eliza was picked up and tossed over a man's shoulder. She heard the gate being unlocked and then a squeak as it opened and closed. After a few steps, Eliza was dropped onto a wooden surface. She landed so hard, she felt her whole side bruising.

A heavy cloth landed across her body. It had the familiar greasy feel of a buffalo hide. Smothered under the hide, she felt more helpless than she ever had in her life. Her wrists were burning from the ropes, and her eyes were filled with dirt. She was breathing fast but not getting enough air. She forced her lungs to slow down. All of Ma's warnings flooded her mind, each worse than the last. Eliza had heard them but had never believed it could happen to her. "I'm sorry, Ma," Eliza whispered, then started to cry.

But Ma wouldn't expect Eliza to just give up. Breathing slowly, in and out, after a few minutes she was able to think clearly. *Who are these men? Are they slave catchers? What are they going to do with me?* She had to pay attention if she was going to get out of this. A horse jangled in its harness. She was in the bed of a wagon, she decided. The wagon shook as the two men climbed onto the wagon seat. A crack of the whip, and they were moving. From the alley next to the Charlesses' house, they turned right—heading away from the city's center. After a few more turns, Eliza lost her bearings. The deserted streets were too quiet to give her any clues to where they were going.

The wagon climbed a hill. Eliza's body started to slide to the back of the wagon. A hand grabbed her and pulled her forward.

"Lie still or you'll regret it," a voice growled above her. It sounded like Amos—the one she had bitten.

Eliza didn't move. Now that she was closer to the driver's seat, she could make out what her abductors were saying.

"Where are we going?" Amos asked.

"We have to meet Bartlett outside the city limits," Jimmy answered.

Reuben Bartlett! The slave catcher had set his sights on her. Eliza almost gave up hope; she was going to the auction block for sure.

The wagon wheels bounced over city cobblestones, then brick and finally dirt. *We must be out of the city by now*, she thought. The wagon stopped and the men jumped out. There was a rumble of indistinguishable voices. Suddenly the weight of the buffalo skin was lifted off her, and she was dragged by her feet from the wagon.

"You better have the right girl," Bartlett warned. The sound of his voice turned Eliza's knees to water. She would have fallen without the rough hands holding her upright.

"If they followed instructions, this is the only girl it can be." The thin nasally voice was familiar too, but Eliza couldn't place it.

Fingers fumbled at her throat, loosening the drawstring. Then with a sharp tug, the bag was pulled from her head. Eliza blinked in the bright light, trying to shield her eyes with her hands. They were in a field of fragrant clover. Two horses were tethered to the wooden fence. She glanced behind her to see a rickety wagon hitched to a broken-down mare. That's how she had been transported. But why here?

"That's her," the second man said.

Eliza's head jerked. "Frank Sanford? You had me kidnapped?"

Frank put his face close enough to hers that she could smell the bourbon on his breath. "It's not kidnapping when you're my property."

Her eyes darting between Bartlett and Frank, Eliza cried, "I was born on the Mississippi River. That means I'm free." She spit in his face. Frank slapped her, but she didn't even flinch. Her cheek stinging, she held her head high.

Bartlett hooked his thumbs in his suspenders and leaned back, examining her like a piece of meat at the butcher. "Slavery goes through the mother. If your ma ain't free, then neither are you."

"You know we're freedom litigants. Mr. Martin told you to leave us alone." The fact that she was here, trussed like a chicken, meant that Bartlett didn't care a hill of beans about Mr. Martin, but Eliza needed time to figure a way out. Her wrists were bound, but her legs were free. Maybe she could run. But she wouldn't get twenty paces with men on horseback chasing her.

Bartlett pulled out a cigar and trimmed it with his knife as though he didn't have a care in the world. "Little girl," he said, "what you don't understand is that a freedom litigant has to abide by the rules. You aren't allowed past the city line, which is about one hundred feet in that direction." He jerked his thumb over his shoulder.

"But I didn't come here willingly," she protested. "You kidnapped me."

Bartlett waved her ideas away. "You are clearly in violation of the court's order. No judge will protect you now. Your rightful owner, Mr. Sanford, can reclaim you."

"It's Mrs. Emerson, the doctor's widow, who owns us!" Eliza couldn't believe these words were coming from her mouth. "No matter what he told you, Frank Sanford has no rights to me at all!"

"Eliza, Eliza," Frank mocked, shaking his head in the most arrogant way possible. "If only that were so. But I have a letter from Auntie. She knew I needed money, so she gave you to me for my birthday." He held out his hands as though it was inevitable. "And I'm selling you to Bartlett here."

Eliza locked her knees to keep from trembling all over. "If that were true, Mr. Bartlett, you wouldn't have to kidnap me!"

"I don't kidnap. I catch fugitives. You were fleeing the city and the court's jurisdiction." He suddenly seemed to lose interest in Eliza. He pulled a wad of banknotes from his pocket and handed it to Frank. "That's what we agreed on."

Frank eagerly counted the money and then carefully put it in his wallet. "It's enough to stake me a gold claim." He handed Bartlett a piece of paper. Without a second glance at Eliza, he walked to his horse and swung up into the saddle. Frank struck the horse with a crop on his flank and sped off toward the city.

With that paper, no one would question Bartlett. Panic threatened to close Eliza's throat, but the rest of her body couldn't stop shaking.

"What are you waiting for?" Bartlett snapped. "Take her to the ship." He paused. "Be careful who sees her. I don't want any trouble with the sheriff. The ship leaves tomorrow at first light, and I'm traveling with it." He headed for his horse.

As Jimmy approached her with the gray sack, Eliza said desperately, "I'm not a slave. I have rights."

Jimmy's answer was a bark of mean laughter.

"If you bring me to my father, he'll give you a reward."

Amos shoved the bag over her head. "As if we'd dare cross Bartlett."

Eliza was picked up and tossed into the wagon like a piece of garbage.

CHAPTER *Twenty*

Eliza was sore in every part of her body. The ropes cut into her skin like a knife. For an instant she almost gave up. Her captors were much stronger than she was. What could a weak girl like her do to save herself?

In the darkness, she imagined Pa's comforting voice saying, *What couldn't a girl like Eliza do?*

She couldn't let Pa down. And what about Ma? All those years of taking such care of Eliza. Was Eliza going to throw that away? No. She was going to get out of this mess and find her way back to her family. But how?

Trying to ignore her bruises and aches, she considered everything she knew. To reach the river, they would have to go down Front Street and then to the northern end of the levee. She wouldn't be far from the shantytown. If Eliza could get out of the wagon, she could lose Jimmy and Amos in the maze of shanties.

First the sack on her head had to be removed. She couldn't

run if she couldn't see. Making only tiny movements, Eliza drew her bound hands to her neck. Her fingers felt the knot of the drawstring. Amos hadn't retied it very tightly, and she was able to loosen it without too much trouble. She was grateful now for the buffalo hide since it concealed what she was doing. Eliza dragged the sack off her head.

She waited until she heard wooden planking rattle under the weight of the wagon. They were at the docks. Sure enough, she heard familiar noises of the ships creaking at their moorings and the birds calling as they swooped over the river. Gently she drew her knees to her chest, catching the buffalo hide between her feet. When she was ready, she could pull the hide off in an instant.

"Which one is it?" Jimmy asked.

"The third one from the north end," Amos said. "And a good thing. There's not many people down here. Remember Bartlett's orders."

"He's always a nasty bastard," Jimmy said. "But lately it's like the devil has him by the tail."

"He needs this shipment to be smooth. He lost money on that girl who died in jail. And since the cholera, there's no auctions."

Eliza braced herself to move when the wagon stopped. Quick as a whip, Eliza yanked the buffalo hide away from her body. She vaulted over the wagon wall, using her bound hands to propel herself off the side of the wagon. Amos shouted a warning to Jimmy. Eliza's legs almost buckled beneath her, but she managed to start running north. Just a little farther and they would never find her in the shantytown. The thudding of footsteps behind her made her run faster. She was close to the first of the shanties. Just a few more yards and she'd be . . .

A heavy hand gripped her shoulder, pulling her backward to the ground.

"No!" Eliza screamed. "Help!"

Eliza tried to crawl away, but Jimmy grabbed her dress, ripping the skirt. Eliza's hand found a branch, and she whacked blindly behind her. Jimmy caught it with his free hand and easily pulled it from her grip. Eliza dug her fingers in the sandy dirt, anything to keep them from taking her. Jimmy finally pinned her arms to her side, her cheek pressed in the dirt. Her eyes full of tears, she saw Amos's feet approach.

"She's a hellcat," Jimmy said, panting.

"I told you," Amos replied. He dropped the buffalo hide to the ground. Together they picked Eliza up. She arched her back and tried to twist out of their grip but they held her down on top of the hide. She kicked at their shins and clawed at their faces, but together they were too strong for her. They rolled her up like a cigar. She was so mad she could spit.

"Bartlett's asking for trouble with this one," Amos said, slamming her body with his booted toe.

"Once she's on board, she's his problem."

Eliza's hands were pressed against her chest so hard they hurt. But the men had made a mistake by leaving her head free. "Help! Help me!" she screamed, until Amos stuffed a foul rag into her mouth. She gagged and threw up a little, but the rag forced the sick back down her throat.

Amos led the way up the gangplank while Jimmy carried Eliza slung over his shoulder. Her head hung upside down and she felt ill. She caught a glimpse of the name on the side of the ship. It was the *Mameluke*.

The *Mameluke* was Wilson's ship! She still had a chance. But the ship was deserted—how could she get a message to him?

Eliza had an idea. Bending her neck and stretching her fingers as far as she could, she caught the end of the precious ribbon Wilson had given her between her fingertips. She tugged it loose. It was Wilson's first and only gift to Eliza; if she could drop it in a place he would see, he would recognize it and come looking for her.

If he was even on board. If he saw it before the ship sailed. If no one tossed it in the river. So many *if*s.

Amos lit a lantern and gestured for Jimmy to go below deck. Eliza dropped the ribbon at the top of the stairs. She felt a little better knowing she'd done something to help herself.

Jimmy lumbered down the narrow stairs, complaining all the way. Eliza's head banged against the railing; she bit her lip rather than give Jimmy the satisfaction of hearing her cry out. They went down another narrower set of stairs to a wooden door with a mortise lock. Amos opened the door.

The room was dark, lit only by the lantern in Amos's hand. Jimmy tossed Eliza onto the floor.

"Take the hide," Amos reminded Jimmy. "It's not our job to give her a fine blanket for her trip."

A mean smile on his face, Jimmy grabbed the edge of the hide and pulled hard. Eliza rolled out, scraping her face against the rough wooden floor. The floor smelled of bilge water and rot. Jimmy handed the hide to Amos, then pulled a big bowie knife from his belt and waved it in front of Eliza's face. She shrank back, staring at the wicked blade.

Jimmy laughed at her. At that moment, she promised herself she wouldn't let them see her afraid again. "If you scream, I'll gut you," he warned. He cut the cloth holding her gag. Eliza spat out the tar-soaked rag.

"Put the shackles on her," Amos directed Jimmy.

A set of shackles was attached to a heavy iron ring in the wall. Eliza tried to stand, but Jimmy shoved her down and fastened a shackle around each leg. They were big on her legs and rubbed her ankles.

"No more running for you," Jimmy gloated.

Eliza's lips and tongue were so dry at first, she could only squawk. She coughed and tried again. "You're in big trouble unless you help me."

Amos and Jimmy exchanged amused looks.

"Is that so?" Jimmy asked.

"I work for Mrs. Charless. Her husband is rich!" Eliza nodded in emphasis. "When the family finds out what you've done, they'll send the sheriff after you. I guarantee it!"

The two men burst out laughing.

"Little girl, who do you think landed you in here?" Jimmy asked.

"What do you mean?" Eliza couldn't keep the confusion from her voice.

"Only Mark Charless—the son of that rich man you're threatening us with. How do you think we knew exactly where you'd be and when? He sent you straight to us."

Eliza slumped against the wall, her shackles weighing on her ankles. She hadn't had time to put it together before, but it made sense. Mark had sent her back on a pointless errand. No one else knew what he had said to her. Then he had driven away while his partner Frank handled the next bit.

"But when they realize I'm missing . . ." Eliza trailed off. She knew what would happen. Mark would say that Eliza had run off to be with her parents. Miss Charlotte and Miss Sofia might even believe it. They knew how frantic Eliza had been to see her family. Ma and Pa wouldn't know for weeks that she was even gone. By then Eliza would be long sold downriver, never to be seen again.

"You can't do this," she cried.

"If I were you, I'd hold your tongue," Amos threatened. "Southern owners don't like slaves who speak their minds."

Jimmy stepped into the hall, and Amos started to close the heavy door.

No matter what it cost her pride, Eliza had to ask, "Aren't you going to leave the light?"

"Not a chance," Amos sneered, rubbing the bite mark

on his arm. "We don't want you burning up this valuable steamboat. Keep quiet or I'll forget what Bartlett said about keeping you unmarked. You understand?"

Eliza nodded sullenly.

The thick wooden door slammed shut, and the key turned in the lock. All that was left was the sound of the wash of the river against the wall behind her and her own ragged breathing.

CHAPTER *Twenty-One*

Eliza's eyes gradually adjusted to the dark. Now she could make out a narrow rectangle high up on the wall that let in a thin line of light and air. The shackles were fastened to a wall, and she could explore only a few feet in either direction. Finally she slid down to the floor, sitting with her back against the wall. Eliza pulled at the knots fastening her hands with her teeth, but the knots were tied too tightly.

She tried to think of what Ma and Pa would do. They wouldn't ever let themselves get into this situation. What about Reverend Meachum? He would pray. But first, he'd make sure that he'd tried everything in his power to help himself. She could always count on one thing to calm her down. Before the panic could overwhelm her, she began to hum. Music always reminded Eliza of happier times, like singing at church or putting Lizzie to sleep with a lullaby.

Think, Eliza, she told herself. She was cargo. There was

no one on this ship who would help her except Wilson. But she couldn't rely on Wilson finding that tiny scrap of ribbon. What else could she do? Her tune got louder, the sound bouncing off the walls. She stopped and listened. She sang a long note and heard it echo back. Could it be that simple? Would her music set her free? Even if Wilson missed the ribbon, he would recognize her voice. He had heard her sing at church. Best of all, if her kidnappers heard, they'd think nothing of it. Just another slave singing a spiritual.

Running her tongue over her lips to moisten her mouth, she took a deep breath and prepared to sing.

> *Amazing Grace, how sweet the sound,*
> *That saved a wretch like me.*
> *I once was lost but now am found,*
> *Was blind, but now I see.*

At first the music was only the tiniest whisper of sound, but soon her voice remembered how to sing out proud and strong:

> *'Twas Grace that taught my heart to fear.*
> *And Grace, my fears relieved.*
> *How precious did that Grace appear,*
> *The hour I first believed.*

Reverend Meachum had told the congregation that a wicked English slave trader, John Newton, wrote the song a hundred years before. He'd realized the evil he had done and sought forgiveness. Now Reuben Bartlett was as far from grace as it was possible to be, so Eliza wouldn't mind if this song was his undoing. And her salvation.

> *Through many dangers, toils and snares,*
> *I have already come;*
> *'Tis Grace that brought me safe thus far,*
> *And Grace will lead me home.*

Before she could start the last verse, she heard two short whistles followed by a longer one. The sound floated from the deck two stories above her head through the narrow window. She waited, holding her breath, until the sequence was repeated. She whistled back, again and again. Finally there was a scratching at the door.

"Eliza?" Wilson's voice was the most welcome sound she'd ever heard.

"Wilson!" Eliza cried, shaking with relief.

"It is you!" he exclaimed. "I recognized your voice. When I went looking, I found your ribbon on the stairs." The door shook on its hinges as he tried to open it. "Why are you locked up in Bartlett's cargo hold?"

"I was kidnapped!" Eliza cried. "They grabbed me from Miss Charlotte's garden and sold me to Bartlett. They *sold* me, Wilson! They stole my life."

"Did they hurt you?" He rattled the door even harder, trying to reach her.

"Not really." Eliza sniffed her runny nose. "They hit me some, but I bit one of them back."

"Good for you!"

"You have to get me out of here!" Eliza cried. "They're going to send me downriver to be sold on the block."

"We won't let that happen," Wilson promised.

Eliza wiped her tears away with her shoulder. "Can you get the key?"

"Bartlett's men keep it," he said.

"There must be another key on the ship." Eliza urged, "Think, Wilson!"

"The captain might have a key."

"Will he help us?" Eliza asked.

"No." Wilson's answer was short and certain. "He gets half his money on every trip from Bartlett and his kind."

"Then you just have to find the key."

There was a silence. "Are you shackled?"

"Yes."

"Even if I find the key to this door . . ." Wilson's voice sounded hopeless. "Only Bartlett's men can open the shackles."

Eliza rotated her sore shoulders and stretched her legs out in front of her. The heavy metal cuffs were rubbing a raw spot on her ankles. "I'll figure out what to do about the shackles," she said. "You just find that key."

From above, someone shouted Wilson's name.

"I'll be back as soon as I can," he promised.

Eliza ran her hands down the chains to her ankles, frantically trying to find a weak link. But they were too strong. She tried the shackle itself. Her fingers slid into the gap between the cold iron and her skin. She twisted her body around to get her hands near her right boot. Every movement scraped her ankle more, but she kept working at it. She untied the lace with her fingertips, then tugged the boot off her foot. As she hoped, the shackle was made for a man's leg, not a girl's. Without the boot, the thick iron ring slipped easily off her foot.

"Bartlett, you think you're so smart," she muttered, as she started on the other foot. "But I won't let you win." A few minutes later, Eliza put her boots back on and double-tied the laces.

She stood up; her unshackled legs felt unsteady. The floor beneath her feet shifted—even docked, the *Mameluke* was at the mercy of the river. A sharp object in her pocket jabbed her in the leg. She felt it with her bound hands—it was Miss Sophie's crochet hook. Mark had used the crochet hooks to trick Eliza, but now a hook was going to free her. Carefully, she tugged at her skirt so she could grab hold of the hook.

Holding the hook between her teeth, Eliza went to work on the rope binding her wrists. The knots were tight and came undone slowly. She worried at every sound in case it was Bartlett or his men. She jumped when a bell clanged from the land side of the boat. Above her head, she heard footsteps and muffled shouts. Getting to her feet, she put her ear to the window. She couldn't make out any words, but she could hear panicked voices.

The rope fell away from her hands. She was free. Where was Wilson? If something was happening on shore, it was the perfect time for Eliza to escape. She went to the narrow window. It was too high for her to see out, but she heard someone shout, "Fire!" In the same instant, she smelled smoke.

Not thinking, she started banging on the door. "Help!" she cried. "Somebody help me!"

"Stop making all that noise." It was Wilson. "Someone will—"

"Did you get the key?" she interrupted, breathless.

"Yes!"

"Thank goodness."

The door swung open, and she leaped into his arms. He hugged her tight. "You're out of the shackles!" he said. "How?"

"Bartlett didn't reckon on a leg as small as mine," she boasted. "Tell me the worst—is the boat on fire?"

"Not ours. The fire started on the *White Cloud.* Then it spread to the *Edward Bates.*"

"Your old ship!"

"It was docked next to us. It's completely ablaze." Wilson's eyes were red-rimmed; Eliza guessed he had shed a tear for his old boat. "They are cutting the mooring ropes so the river can take it far from the other boats."

She wanted to comfort Wilson, but there was no time.

"This is my chance to get off the ship while everyone's watching the fire," she said.

Wilson agreed. He brought out a pair of trousers, a shirt, and a cap. "They won't be looking for a boy."

Eliza beamed. "Turn your back so I can change."

Obediently he faced away. The clothes were too big, but she could move in them. She threw the dress in the corner of her cell; she had never liked slave blue anyway.

The shouting on deck grew louder. Eliza and Wilson froze and listened. But they were caught off guard when the *Mameluke* shook, throwing Eliza to the ground.

"Wilson?" Her voice was small and frightened. "What happened?"

He pulled her to her feet. "We have to go. Now."

"What was that noise?" she asked.

"I'm afraid the *Edward Bates* just floated into our ship." Grabbing her hand, he headed for the stairs. "If we aren't on fire yet, we soon will be."

CHAPTER *Twenty—Two*

WILSON SPED UP THE NARROW STAIRS, ELIZA CLOSE BEHIND him. It was too dark to make out what was happening above. Somehow the sun had set while she'd been locked up in that cell. There was a loud explosion, and the sky lit up like fireworks.

Wilson poked his head above deck. He returned, almost falling down the stairs. "The deck is burning," he cried. "We have to get off another way."

"How?" Eliza asked.

Wilson pointed down a corridor that led to the back of the boat. "Hurry!"

Eliza ran to the end of the hallway. There was a hatch in the center of the wall.

"Push it open!" Wilson yelled.

She shoved and the hatch swung open from a hinge at the top. She poked her head out. They were above the paddle wheel at the rear of the *Mameluke*. Even though the sun had set, there was a red glow that lit up the river. Above her, she heard snapping and cracking. The fire had touched the sky, sending sparks floating down in front of them. She could see the flames licking the top of the boat.

Screams from the front were followed by splashes. Eliza grabbed Wilson's arm. "The crew's jumping!" she shouted.

Wilson bellowed in her ear, "We can climb down from here."

A narrow wooden ladder was attached to one side of the hatch. She stared at the water. "I can't! It's too high!" she cried.

"Eliza, you have to!" Wilson insisted. "There's a dinghy for us down there." He tilted her chin so she had to look him straight in the eye. "A little ladder can't stop Eliza Scott, right?"

She shook her head.

"I'll go first, then you follow. One foot down, then another. All right?"

Behind her the smoke had reached the corridor.

Unable to speak, she nodded.

"Good." Wilson descended quickly.

Eliza hesitated. If only the ladder weren't so small and the water so far below. A wave of heat rushed down the narrow corridor. The walls were already streaked with fire. She was out of time.

"Eliza, you must come now!" Wilson called.

She took a deep breath and climbed onto the ladder. She locked her fingers around the top rung; it was slick and cold.

First one foot down, then the other. "Don't look down. Don't look down." She chanted it over and over like a prayer. The huge paddle wheel creaked next to her. She closed her mind to everything but Wilson's voice. Finally her foot hit a flat surface. She let go of the ladder and fell to the platform. "I did it!"

A small dinghy was turned upside down on the narrow platform near the paddle wheel. Together they heaved and flipped the rowboat into the water. While Wilson prepared the oars, Eliza stared at the levee. The fire brigade was already there fighting the blaze. The captain, with his distinctive helmet, shouted into a metal trumpet that made his voice loud enough for his men to hear, but their efforts were useless. The next boat down from the *Mameluke* was already on fire.

"Get in." Wilson steadied the boat.

"I want to go to my parents!" Eliza said. "No slave catcher will look for me in jail."

"First we have to steer clear of the boat. We'll fight our way ashore once we're past the fire."

A large piece of flaming wood fell, hissing as it hit the river.

"Hurry!" Wilson jumped into the boat and grabbed the oars. With strong, sure pulls, he brought the rowboat away from the *Mameluke* into the open channel beyond the burning boats. The wind was strong, pushing them toward the shore. Eliza clapped her hands over her ears to shut out the crackling and hissing sounds of the fire.

Her back to shore, Eliza twisted to see the flames. The *White Cloud* had burned down to the water and the *Mameluke* was almost gone, only the great paddle still standing. She swallowed hard. Trapped in the bowels of that ship—she would have been dead by now without Wilson. She gripped the seat beneath her. The splintered wood felt real to her and somehow convinced her that she was still alive. She was finally safe . . . she hoped.

The *Edward Bates*, still adrift, bumped into boats farther down the levee, spreading the fire as it went. Already a dozen boats were burning. Behind them, the giant paddle wheel of the *Mameluke* burst into flame.

"Hurry, Wilson," Eliza shouted. "We have to get to shore."

"There's nowhere safe to land on the St. Louis side," Wilson yelled.

"Then where can we go?"

The fire reflected in his eyes as he measured the distance across the river. "I might be able to row us to the other side."

"I'm not allowed to leave St. Louis! It will look like I'm running to Illinois."

"We have to save ourselves. Be sensible, Eliza!"

"I can't cross the river!" Eliza cried. "What about heading upstream? There's no fire there."

"The current's too fast. I can't fight that by myself. And if we stay here, the wind will take us into the flames."

"We can't go ashore. We can't cross. We can't stay." Eliza pleaded, "What can we do?"

A boat exploded. For an instant, the entire river lit up. Just when it seemed they had no options, Eliza spotted a familiar ship moored in the river. It was like an answer to a prayer. Why hadn't she thought of it earlier?

"Take us to the *Freedom School*!"

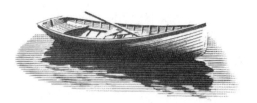

CHAPTER *Twenty-Three*

"THAT'S THE PERFECT PLACE," WILSON AGREED QUICKLY. "We'll be far enough from the fire there." Eliza could see the relief in his face. She understood how afraid he had been.

Rowing with one oar, Wilson turned the boat. The current caught their dinghy with a rush, and water crashed into the boat. At first Eliza thought it was just water coming in over the side; then she realized the water was pooling in the bottom.

"The boat's leaking!" Eliza shouted.

"How bad?"

"Bad. And it's getting worse."

"Bail quicker!" Wilson ordered, rowing hard.

Eliza slipped onto her knees so she could get rid of the water faster. Her trousers were soon soaked through, and her whole body felt numb from the cold water. She kept scooping and tossing the water overboard. Once the water level dropped she could see feel a hole in the side of the boat. "I found the hole!" she said.

"Can you plug it closed?" Wilson's voice was stretched thin.

Using her teeth, she tore off a piece of her shirt and twisted it into the hole. The water slowed. Breathing hard, she closed her eyes.

"Eliza, talk to me!" Wilson begged.

"I think I stopped it," she panted. She climbed back onto the seat.

The easterly wind chilled her even through her thick shirt. The farther they got from the shore, the darker it was. She couldn't hear the fire anymore over the sharp wind.

The boat suddenly lurched and began to spin around.

"What's happening?" Eliza cried, feeling dizzy.

Wilson got the boat pointed in the direction of the school. "We're hitting the main river," he announced. Out of the channel where the boats were docked, the Mississippi ran faster and stronger. "Keep a sharp eye out."

"For what?" Eliza croaked, exhaustion and smoke roughening her voice.

"Debris . . . comes down . . . the river," he said between gasping breaths. "It's too dark . . . for me to see it. Take that extra oar . . . and be ready to push off anything . . . that might hit the boat." He didn't need to say that the boat already had one leak and that another one might sink them.

They were out in the deepest part of the current when Eliza cried, "I see something!"

"Where?" he asked, craning his neck to look behind him.

"There!" Eliza pointed upriver. "It's big and heading straight for us!" She held the oar in front of her like a weapon.

"It's a tree!"

"Watch out!" Wilson shouted, trying to maneuver them out of the way.

The tree came at them fast. Eliza shoved it away from their boat with her oar, but a branch scraped against the bottom of the rowboat. Eliza winced at the sound, praying it hadn't pierced another hole in the boat. After a few moments, she decided that they had been lucky and the boat was still river-worthy.

"We're almost there," Wilson hollered. He rowed hard to break free of the current.

Eliza looked up to see the *Freedom School* riding high and proud on its mooring. She blinked back tears. The school had always been special, but tonight it would save their lives. Near the island, the water was calmer, giving Wilson a needed rest. The little boat finally bumped into the side of the *Freedom School*, and Eliza pulled them to safety.

"We made it!" she cried. She climbed out of the boat, forcing her tired muscles to move. Wilson threw her the line. Her frozen hands were clumsy but she managed to tie up the boat. Wilson bent over, struggling to catch his breath. Finally he looked up with a tired grin. "I'm going to have to teach you to tie a better knot."

Eliza laughed. "After everything we've been through,

you're complaining about my knots?" She retrieved the key from its hiding spot under a coiled rope and unlocked the door to the classroom. Inside, the relief from the wind was a blessing. Eliza hadn't noticed until then that her ears ached from the cold.

"Are there any blankets?" Wilson asked.

Eliza nodded. "Sometimes the reverend lets people stay here if they have no other place to go." She opened a cabinet at the end of the schoolroom and pulled out some pallets and blankets. They took two blankets each and returned to the deck. They sat with their backs to the wall, facing the docks. In the time it had taken them to get to the *Freedom School*, the fire had spread to even more boats.

"Do you think my family is safe?" Eliza asked.

"Yes," he answered. "The fire is only at the river."

But Eliza couldn't see the levee through the wall of flame linked by the docked ships. Or what was left of them.

"Twenty-one, twenty-two, twenty-three boats," Wilson counted. "All gone. And my *Edward Bates* along with it."

"They'll rebuild it," Eliza said.

"I hope so."

"If it weren't for you, I'd have gone down with the *Mameluke*," Eliza said softly, her eyes fixed on the opposite shore. A tremor went through her body. "No one else would have saved me."

He put his hand over hers. "I'd do anything for you," he said simply.

His words were a vow of sorts. Eliza didn't think twice

before she answered, "I feel the same way."

Eliza waited for him to say something else—but then she realized that he'd fallen asleep. She adjusted his blanket around his shoulders. She lay her head against him and watched the fire.

Without the heat and sounds of the fire, the burning levee looked more like a painting than real life. After a while the fire ran out of boats. Maybe now it would die, she hoped. They had lost enough tonight.

Eliza's heart tightened when she spotted figures on shore frantically pulling bundles from the fire. The fire had spread to the docks, and the next day's cargo, huge piles of hemp and tobacco, was being consumed by flames. Even from across the river, she could smell the burning tobacco. She knew she should feel horrified or sad, but instead she felt tired. Everything that had happened today had used her up. She had nothing left inside for worrying.

A wagon loaded high with crates burst into flames. In a moment, the flames had jumped from the wagon to the warehouse behind it and then rapidly from one warehouse to another. Within minutes the first warehouse collapsed, and Eliza saw the fire flare up in the buildings behind the row of warehouses. The fire wasn't satisfied with the port—it wanted the city too. And that meant . . .

Suddenly, Eliza realized she still had some room left to be feel scared. "Wilson! Wake up!" Eliza jumped to her feet and ran to the railing.

"What's wrong?" Wilson jerked awake.

"The fire is spreading into the city. What if it spreads to the jail? What about Ma and Pa?" Her eyes strained to make out the dome of the courthouse; it was just barely visible floating above the smoke and fire.

"Eliza, the jail is almost a mile inland." Wilson got to his feet, groaning with fatigue. "A long ways off from the fire."

"It could spread." She pulled him to the railing and pointed at the dome. "They're locked in the jail. I have to warn them."

"We'd never make it in the dark. Not with that leak. We can go in the morning."

"But my family . . ."

He tried to pull her away from the railing, but she held on tightly. "The alarms went off a long time ago—everyone in town knows there's a fire. It won't get as far as the jail, and even if it did, your ma and pa have plenty of time to get out." Wilson draped a blanket back around her.

Eyes fixed on the fire line, all Eliza could do was watch the flames slowly engulf the buildings. Everything they touched, they destroyed. Each block the fire burned was filled with people's houses and businesses. Off to the north side, she saw the shantytown go up in a whoosh of fire that she could hear even from the deck of the *Freedom School*. Eliza's chest ached. She knew what it was like to lose a home. When Mrs. Emerson had forced her family to move to the jail, they'd lost the little house they'd rented for years.

"I should be with them," Eliza insisted weakly.

"You won't be of any use to anybody tonight. You need to

rest." Wilson pressed her shoulders down so she would sit. "I don't know how you can still stand after the day you've had."

"It's my fault I'm not there," she said. "If I'd listened to my ma, none of this would have happened."

"Did you cause the fire too?" Wilson asked. "I mean, as long as you're taking the blame for everything."

"Don't make fun of me. I'm trying to take responsibility for what I did."

"Not one girl in a hundred could do what you did today." Eliza felt a lump rise in her throat. "You should be proud of yourself," he finished.

"But it was my fault to begin with," Eliza protested.

"The blame for what happened isn't yours. It's slavery that's at fault. When we fix that, everything will be better." He settled back against the wall and put his arm around Eliza. She leaned into the crook of his shoulder.

"Someday I'll be free. Free to write my music."

"And go to school."

"And travel up and down the Mississippi—and who knows? Maybe go even farther."

Nestled under his arm, she felt him drop a kiss on the top of her head. "We'll go together," Wilson agreed.

All the aches and bruises that ailed Eliza's body faded away. She said nothing but inside she was singing.

"I forgot to give this back to you," he said, pulling something out of his pocket with his other hand.

"My ribbon," Eliza whispered. "You kept it."

She took it from him and tied it to her braid. "Now I have

a pair again." He squeezed her tight. After a few minutes, she heard his breathing change and he was fast asleep.

The waterfront was destroyed and the fire was still spreading. Eliza and her family weren't freed yet. Men like Bartlett, Mark Charless, and Frank Sanford would most likely never be brought to account for their crimes. It was enough to make Eliza cry.

But, on the other hand, she'd saved herself today. Wilson had proved to be someone she could depend on, just like Ma and Pa could depend on each other. And he wanted a future with her. Tomorrow she'd find her family, and they would start anew. Even as she watched St. Louis burn, Eliza decided that maybe the future had a chance. Quietly, so as not to wake Wilson, she began to sing.

> *I was born on the river in the pouring rain,*
> *And wandering is my middle name.*
> *As long as I live, my strength I will give*
> *To the river that's never the same.*

Epilogue

"Today is the day?" Lizzie asked.

"Today is the day," Eliza promised.

The Scotts' court date had finally arrived. Their lawyer had promised that the papers were ready, the witnesses were prepared, and, most importantly of all, the judge and jury were there to hear the case.

Much had changed in St. Louis in the past seven months. By November the cholera had left as quickly as it had arrived. The disease had claimed over four thousand lives in the city, but thankfully none of Eliza's loved ones.

"I'm cold," Lizzie complained.

Eliza pulled off her new coat and draped it around her sister's shoulders. "Now hush, Lizzie. As soon as Mr. Hall arrives, we'll go into the courtroom. It's warmer there."

Ma and Pa were sitting on a bench on the plaza, holding

hands. Eliza thought they looked like the courting couple they must have been once. Ma's face was worried, as usual, but Pa seemed confident.

"Eliza, your friends are here," Pa said, tilting his chin toward the far side of the courthouse plaza.

Eliza hurried to meet Wilson and Celia. "You didn't have to come!" She greeted them with wide-open arms.

"We wouldn't miss this," Wilson assured her. There had been plenty of construction work for Wilson to do after the fire, and he had grown at least two inches in the past half year. His shoulders were bulky with new muscles. At Reverend Meachum's invitation, he was living on the *Freedom School* with a dozen other people displaced by the fire. He teased Eliza that now he'd read even more books than she. He'd just found a job with a new steamboat that would be making the journey between St. Louis and Hannibal weekly. Every Sunday he came to church with the Scotts and had dinner with them in their small house not far from the river. Mr. Hall had finally convinced the court to let the Scotts leave the prison.

Celia grinned. "I wanted to come too," she said. "Although I'm not exactly sure what's happening."

"I'll explain," Eliza promised.

The three friends sat on the low wall at the edge of the plaza. The winter sun was dazzlingly bright. They could easily see all of downtown St. Louis, the river, and beyond. "You can even see the *Freedom School* from here," Eliza said. Celia had joined their classes and was becoming a fair student.

"The levee is as full of boats as it ever was," Wilson said. "It's hard to believe that the fire destroyed it all."

The fire had destroyed fifteen of the city's blocks, including Eliza's favorite music store. But the jail had been spared as well as Reverend Meachum's church. The warehouses and other downtown buildings were being rebuilt with brick or other materials that could withstand a fire.

"Not everything's being rebuilt," Celia said a bit sourly. Her eyes were resting on the area where the shantytown had been. Even though Celia and her ma lived in a proper house now, she was still bitter that the fire brigades hadn't tried to save the shantytown.

Mr. Hall, wearing a sharp brown suit, approached, taking the steps two at a time. "Dred!" he called out. "It's time."

"That's our lawyer, Mr. Hall," Eliza explained. They filed in behind Mr. Hall and Eliza's parents. Lizzie was perched on Pa's hip. A few other people trailed in too. They weren't connected with the Scotts, but they were here to watch the proceedings. Eliza had heard that for murder trials the courtroom was filled with spectators. But the Scotts' little case, no matter how important it was to them, didn't attract much of an audience.

Eliza had been only nine the last time she'd been in the courthouse, but she'd never forgotten the courtroom. There was a raised bench where the judge's chair was. White columns lined the room underneath an arched ceiling with a skylight. "That's where the jury sits," she said to Celia, pointing to the raised box along the right side of the courtroom. "And the judge will be there. Ma and Pa will sit with Mr. Hall. We'll sit behind them."

The bailiff brought in the jury, twelve white men who took their seats with a serious air. Some of them stared at Eliza's family. She stared back. Maybe if they understood that a real family was at stake, they would do the right thing.

"Why would twelve white men ever give you your freedom?" Celia asked suspiciously. "What's in it for them?"

"They aren't giving us anything. They'll follow the law. It's the law that sets us free," Eliza explained. She crossed her fingers and sent up a little prayer. "Once I have my freedom papers, men like Bartlett can't take me again."

Eliza still got the shivers when she thought about Bartlett. Mr. Hall had sent the sheriff after Bartlett for kidnapping, but the slave catcher had left town. He was still hunting slaves, but at least he was doing it somewhere else. Eliza took comfort knowing she'd never see him again.

The courtroom doors opened and Miss Charlotte came in. Miss Charlotte had been appalled when she heard what her son had done to Eliza. But Mark and Frank had left for California before anyone could punish them for kidnapping. Eliza had heard that they hadn't found any gold, and their appeals for more money met deaf ears at home.

Miss Charlotte walked up to Pa and shook his hand. "Dred, I wish you good luck."

"Thank you, Miss Charlotte," he said. "We appreciate all your help."

Miss Charlotte nodded and had turned to leave when she

glimpsed Eliza. She beckoned and Eliza came to her.

"How are you, Eliza?" Miss Charlotte asked.

"Very well, thank you," Eliza answered.

"Aunt Sofia wanted to be here today, but her rheumatism is acting up," Miss Charlotte told her. "She hounded me until I promised to come and support you."

"Thank you, ma'am," Eliza said politely. "I'll be back tomorrow." Ma wouldn't let Eliza live at the Charlesses' house, but she had agreed to let Eliza keep caring for Miss Sofia. Now that Mark was gone, working there was much better. Eliza was quite happy seeing her family at night but being apart from them by day.

The bailiff entered the courtroom and bellowed, "All rise. The St. Louis Circuit Court is now in session, the Honorable Alexander Hamilton presiding." Everyone stood. Eliza watched the jury intently. Her fate was in their hands, and she didn't even know their names.

Despite the importance of the day, the proceedings were quite dull. Celia soon fell asleep as the morning dragged on with conversation between the lawyers, the judge, and the witnesses who had known Dr. Emerson when Dred Scott was his slave.

Finally, the judge said it was time for the jury to make a decision. The twelve men filed out of the courtroom.

The Scotts went outside and ate the lunch they had brought. It was cold but the sun was shining. Conversations started and then sputtered away. Each one of them knew that their futures were being decided at that very moment. Eliza's stomach felt tight from too much hoping and worrying. Even the cake Wilson had brought tasted like ash.

Mr. Hall came to find them. "They have a verdict."

When the jury filed into the courtroom, they did not look at the Scotts. Eliza wanted to ask Pa if that meant anything, but one glance at him and she held her tongue. Pa was standing tall, his back straight and his head held high. Ma's hand clutched his. Lizzie hid her face in Eliza's skirt.

Wilson whispered in Eliza's ear, "You're going to win."

Eliza stared straight ahead, wishing harder than she'd ever wished before. She felt her heart racing as though even her blood were impatient too.

"Jury," asked the judge, "do you have a verdict?"

The man in the front of the jury box stood. "We do, Your Honor."

"Please hand your determination to the bailiff."

The bailiff took a folded paper to the judge. He read it and asked the jury, "Do you all agree?" The twelve men nodded.

Eliza couldn't sit still; her foot tapped uncontrollably. She closed her eyes and hummed silently until the judge read aloud from the paper in his hand. Eliza couldn't take in the meaning of the words. But it was clear they'd won from the way Mr. Hall slapped Pa on the back. Ma smiled broadly, tears running down her cheeks.

"We won?" Eliza asked.

"You're free," Wilson said. He picked up Eliza and twirled her around in a circle.

"We won!" Eliza cried, brushing tears off her cheeks.

"Congratulations!" Celia burst out.

Eliza sank down in her seat. "Free!"

Mr. Hall walked over to the bailiff. He came back with the piece of paper the judge had read. "Here's your verdict," he said. "Would you like me to read it to you?"

Eliza started to speak, then stopped herself. Ma noticed and squeezed Eliza's hand. "Maybe Eliza can read it to us?"

Startled, Eliza met her ma's gaze.

"No one can stop you now," Ma whispered to Eliza.

"I'd like that," Eliza said.

Mr. Hall handed the paper to Eliza with a ceremony that felt right for the occasion. Eliza took it with trembling hands. The words in spiky handwriting represented her whole future. A future that she could choose for herself.

She began to read aloud because she was free to do so.

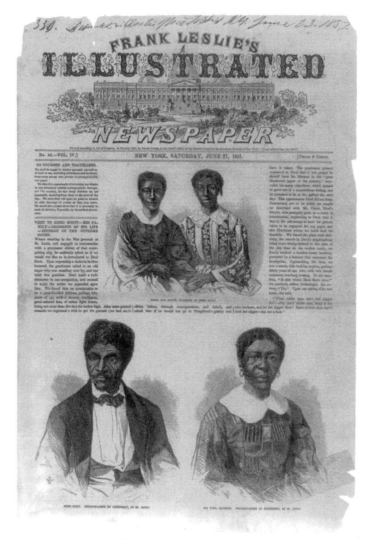

The Dred Scott family on the cover of *Frank Leslie's Illustrated Newspaper* in 1857, the year they lost their Supreme Court case

Authors' Note

THE DRED SCOTT DECISION

At the end of *Freedom's Price*, the Scott family finally won their freedom. Unfortunately, they did not keep it for long. Mrs. Emerson appealed the decision in less than a month. The Scotts' legal battle continued for another eight years until they lost in the United States Supreme Court in 1857. Chief Justice Roger Taney, a Virginia slaveholder, declared their suit invalid because no person of African descent could ever be a U.S. citizen. The judge also declared the Missouri Compromise of 1820 unconstitutional, which meant that the federal government could no longer prohibit slavery in the territories. The *Dred Scott* decision outraged abolitionists and is viewed as one of the reasons for the outbreak of the American Civil War in April 1861.

While Mrs. Emerson ultimately won her case, her circumstances had changed over the eleven years it took for the case to be decided. She'd married Dr. Calvin C. Chaffee in 1850.

Dr. Chaffee was a politician with abolitionist views and was a member of the U.S. House of Representatives from 1855 to 1859. Once Mrs. Emerson married him, her property became his—so ironically, an abolitionist politician owned the most notorious slave family in the country. After the Supreme Court ruled against the Scotts, Dr. Chaffee immediately freed the Scotts on May 26, 1857.

THE SCOTT FAMILY

We do not know a great deal about the Scott family. Since Harriet and Dred couldn't read or write, they left very few records behind. Dred and Harriet did meet in the Wisconsin Territory and were married there. In St. Louis, Dred worked in Mr. Hall's office. Harriet was a laundress who would have washed her clothes along the banks of the Mississippi.

The St. Louis levee in the mid- to late 1800s

Miss Charlotte's family, the Charlesses, did own Dred at one time before selling him to Dr. Emerson. And they supported the Scotts' lawsuit. The Scott family was forced to live in a jail while their case was being heard. In May 1849 the cholera epidemic caused their case to be postponed yet again. They survived the epidemic and the Great Fire of 1849. Eliza's adventures are fictional, although the terrors she faced were very real threats to a black girl in St. Louis, Missouri, in 1849.

Dred was a small man and seems to have been charming and well liked. He died of tuberculosis in September 1858, less than two years after he formally gained his freedom. He was around fifty-nine years old. His wife, Harriet, was illiterate but was most likely the driving force behind Dred Scott's lawsuit. She was a devoted churchwoman and known for her fine character. Around twenty years younger than her husband, she lived very quietly after his death, taking in laundry. In her old age, Harriet became a house servant, a less physically demanding job, until her death in June 1876 at the age of around sixty-one.

Eliza married Wilson Madison sometime before 1863. Eliza was probably around twenty-four when she married (in *Freedom's Price*, we made Eliza a little older than she was in real life in 1849). She worked as a laundress for her entire life. Wilson achieved his dream and became a pastry chef. They had six children, but only two sons survived, Harry and John. Wilson died in May 1881 at age forty-three, and Eliza died the next year. She was also forty-three.

Lizzie Scott's life was a bit of a mystery. She never married, and even though she lived in St. Louis, she seemed to have lost touch with her family. After Eliza's death, her sons Harry and John (ages twelve and nine) were orphaned. According to family lore, the two boys sat on a curb holding their only possession—a charcoal drawing of Dred and Harriet. A woman they did not know passed them on the street, recognized the drawing, and took in the two boys. She raised them but never mentioned that she was, in fact, their aunt, Lizzie Scott. She lived until 1945, when she died of pneumonia at the age of ninety-nine. There are still Scott family descendants through Eliza and Wilson's son John.

MUSIC

Eliza's love of singing is an important part of *Freedom's Price*. In the 1840s singing was one of the few forms of free entertainment available to African Americans. It was an important part of their culture, both at church and at home. Eliza's ambition to be a songwriter would have been unusual but not impossible. "The Blue Juniata," the song Eliza sings to Miss Sofia, was a popular song written by Marion Dix Sullivan. The song that Eliza composes throughout the story is fictional.

THE CHOLERA EPIDEMIC AND THE GREAT FIRE OF 1849

The cholera epidemic in 1849 claimed more than 4,500 lives in St. Louis. Cholera is a bacterial abdominal infection caused by contaminated food and water. There was no known cure in the mid-1800s. Today we realize that cholera can be

A print of the Great Fire at St. Louis, Thursday night, May 17, 1849

prevented with proper sanitation, but in the 1840s little was known about the disease. Dred Scott was ahead of his time when he advised his family to wash their hands and to only drink clean water.

The St. Louis Great Fire of May 17, 1849, started on a paddle-wheeled steamboat, the *White Cloud*. The flames jumped to its neighbor, the *Edward Bates*. The *Edward Bates* was cut free from the dock, but the wind and current pushed it back into the levee. Within thirty minutes, a total of twenty-three steamboats had caught fire.

The fire lasted almost twelve hours, traveling slowly from the warehouse district along the levee through the downtown commercial district. Remarkably, there were only three recorded deaths, including Fire Captain Thomas Targee. To save the great St. Louis Cathedral, Captain Targee blew up several buildings to create a firebreak. One of these buildings was Eliza's beloved music store. The firebreak was successful, but Targee died in his own explosion. Altogether 415 buildings were destroyed. The jail, the Charlesses' house, and the Baptist Church were spared. The shantytown where Celia and her mother once lived was completely destroyed.

OTHER PEOPLE IN *FREEDOM'S PRICE*

Reuben Bartlett was one of the most notorious slave catchers of the time. While the *Mameluke* did travel between St. Louis and New Orleans, we don't know if Bartlett used it. Eliza's kidnapping was invented, but it was common practice for unscrupulous slave catchers to grab African Americans off the street and sell them into slavery.

Reverend John Berry Meachum started life as a slave, then purchased freedom for himself, his family, and many others with money earned from his skilled woodworking. He was educated and formally trained as a minister. Meachum started a school for African Americans in the basement of the Baptist Church. When he encountered local opposition, he moved the school to a steamboat he had built and anchored in federal waters on the Illinois side of the Mississippi River. Missouri law didn't apply in the middle of the river. Both that school and the steamboat were known as the *Freedom School*.

Mrs. Charless did help the Scotts with their lawsuit. It was her brother, Taylor Blow, who helped Dr. Chaffee eventually free the family. The Scotts' owner, Mrs. Emerson, was part of the prominent Sanford family. However, Mark Charless and his friend Frank Sanford are invented characters, as is Miss Sofia. After gold was discovered in California, it became popular for young men to seek their fortune in the gold fields. Most were not successful.

A Note about Our Sources / Further Reading[*]

THE SCOTT FAMILY

There are many books written about the *Dred Scott* case. There are fewer books about the Scotts as a family. We relied on these:

Hager, Ruth Ann (Abels). *Dred & Harriet Scott: Their Family Story.* St. Louis, MO: St. Louis County Library, 2010.
Ms. Hager is a reference specialist in St. Louis County Library's Special Collections Department, which focuses on family and local history. She is also a certified genealogist and lecturer on genealogy.

Moses, Sheila. *I, Dred Scott.* New York: Simon and Schuster's Children's Books, 2005.
A fictionalized slave narrative based on the life and legal precedent of Dred Scott. The book has a foreword by John A. Madison Jr., a great-grandson of Dred Scott.

*websites active at time of publication

Swain, Gwenyth. *Dred and Harriet Scott: A Family's Struggle for Freedom*. St. Paul, MN: Borealis Books, 2004.
A carefully researched family biography that begins with Dred's childhood on a Virginia plantation and continues with his later travels to Alabama, Missouri, Illinois, and the territory that would become Minnesota. The author explores the power of the Scott family ties and the severe challenges that Dred and Harriet faced as they fought for freedom for Eliza and Lizzie.

VanderVelde, Lea. *Mrs. Dred Scott: A Life on Slavery's Frontier*. New York: Oxford University Press, 2009.
An extraordinary biography about Harriet Scott, an illiterate woman who grew up in the nation's frontier. VanderVelde uses her research on the time period to piece together what Harriet's life might have been like.

Other useful resources about the Scott family include the following:

Charles River Editors. *American Legends: The Life of Dred Scott and the Dred Scott Decision*. Cambridge, MA: CreateSpace Independent Publishing Platform, 2013.

Dred Scott Heritage Foundation. http://www.thedredscottfoundation.org/dshf/.

Missouri State Archives. "Missouri's Dred Scott Case, 1846–1857." http://www.sos.mo.gov/archives/resources/ africanamerican/scott/scott.asp.

LIFE ON THE MISSISSIPPI RIVER

The Mississippi River played a crucial role in Eliza's life as we have interpreted it. The river also played an important role in the city of St. Louis in the nineteenth century. The following three books offer a good background about life on the Mississippi River during this time period:

Buchanan, Thomas C. *Black Life on the Mississippi: Slaves, Free Blacks, and the Western Steamboat World.* Chapel Hill: University of North Carolina Press, 2004.
A well-written book that focuses on black workers, both enslaved and free, on the Mississippi during the nineteenth century.

Gillespie, Michael. *Come Hell or High Water: A Lively History of Steamboating on the Mississippi and Ohio Rivers.* Stoddard, WI: Heritage Press, 2001.
A general history of steamboats on two major rivers. Since St. Louis was such an important location on the Mississippi, that city comes in for a fair amount of coverage in this book.

Sandlin, Lee. *Wicked River: The Mississippi When It Last Ran Wild.* New York: Pantheon Books, 2010.

This book covers the entire history of the river, with a particular focus on the development of commerce on the river during the nineteenth century.

THE ST. LOUIS CHOLERA EPIDEMIC AND THE GREAT FIRE OF 1849

The *St. Louis Post-Dispatch* (www.stltoday.com) is a local newspaper with several interesting articles about the cholera epidemic and the Great Fire of 1849. You might also check out articles in the *St. Louis Magazine* (www.stlmag.com) or the *Southeast Missourian* (www.semissourian.com). Search for "Cholera 1849" or "Great Fire 1849."

A comprehensive survey of historical information about St. Louis, including a list of websites, can be found at the St. Louis Community Information Network (http://stlcin. missouri.org/history/). The website of the Missouri History Museum is also useful (http://www.mohistory.org/).

Photo Credits

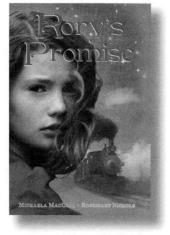